"What were you doing before I woke up?" she asked to cover her confusion.

"Oh, just a little whittling. I find it helps pass the time." He rose and retrieved the object he had been working on. "Here, I did this for you," he said as he held the piece of wood out to her. "Hummingbirds are incredibly beautiful and delicate, yet also strong and independent," he explained. "Like you." His voice had become husky.

Julie looked down at the bird. Its face reminded her of the festival mask he had selected for her from Madame Lucie's collection. The vision of making love to him, the wolf, flooded back. At the time she had found arousing the sense of anonymity the masks provided. Had it only been two days ago?

Last night there had been no masks. For the first time they had come together honestly—two people, no more or no less than who they really were. Her body stirred with the memory.

Matt hadn't let go of the bird when she went to take it from him and his hands melded with the textures of the carving. She stroked the hummingbird's extended wings, feeling its feathers morph into gentle fingertips. Its head and neck were smooth, Matt's hands strong and hard.

"Did you know some hummingbirds' wings beat
red times per second?" he whispered. "Can

wly. She had raised her gaze to
herself in his eyes. They
sure she had an
ngbird's wings beat
eeping pace with her
h and closed her eyes

Acclaim for Brenda Gayle

SOLDIER FOR LOVE placed second in the 2006 Ottawa Romance Writers Association's First Meet contest.

Linda
Bonsoir!
Brenda Gayle

Soldier for Love

by

Brenda Gayle

This is a work of fiction. Names, characters, places, and incidents are either the product of the author's imagination or are used fictitiously, and any resemblance to actual persons living or dead, business establishments, events, or locales, is entirely coincidental.

Soldier for Love

Contact Information: info@thewildrosepress.com

Cover Art by *Rae Monet*

The Wild Rose Press
PO Box 708
Adams Basin, NY 14410-0708
Visit us at www.thewildrosepress.com

Publishing History
Last Rose of Summer Edition, 2008
Print ISBN 1-60154-401-4

Published in the United States of America

Dedication

For Rosemary, who convinced me I should.
And especially for Bruce, who always knew I could.

CHAPTER 1

The Hercules aircraft hit the runway with a body-wrenching *thwump*. The whine of metal-on-metal pierced the throbbing monotony of the rumbling engine as the brakes strove to slow the plane.

The force of the landing pinned Major Julie Collins back in her seat, although it didn't stop her from being jostled from side to side as the metal mammoth bumped and ground its way along the pitted runway.

It hadn't been a long flight—just three hours from Pope Air Force Base in North Carolina to Port-au-Paix, the capital of Beljou Island in the heart of the Caribbean Sea—but to Julie the journey seemed interminable. She tried to use the time to review her notes and listen to what Murray was telling her about their assignment, but she couldn't concentrate.

The hairs on her neck bristled and she could feel his eyes boring into the back of her seat. She checked the pile of documents again. There were no details about any of the troops in the plane, only their pictures, names and ranks arranged as a sort of family tree with her at the head. And there he was staring back at her—Matthew Wolf, Lieutenant.

What is he doing here? she wondered for the hundredth time.

There had been a numbing chill in the pre-dawn air as Julie and Master Sergeant Murray had entered the hanger for a quick inspection of the troops before they boarded the flight. She shivered, not as much from the cold as from the excitement of her first overseas command.

As they rounded the aircraft to approach the parade of troops there had been something all-too-familiar about one of the soldiers. He was taller than the others and had an air of self-assurance that was impossible to mistake. As they drew closer, she saw clearly the well-defined line of the jaw that she had nuzzled just a few hours before, and remembered that her fingers had run along his cheek, down to those... lips.

Her stomach lurched, and she had stumbled slightly. Murray put out a hand to steady her and he had given her a funny look—not concern, exactly.

Her mind had raced with questions as she'd walked down the line to formally acknowledge the hundred or so troops she would be commanding. Julie knew all of them, if not personally, at least by sight—all except for four. Matt and three other men stood at the end of the first row, slightly separate from the rest of the group. Even their uniforms identified them as different; each wore the distinctive maroon berets of paratroopers.

"Lieutenant Matthew Wolf," he had said when she stopped in front of him. He stood to attention and saluted smartly, but his eyes were fixed on some spot over her shoulder. "Communications."

She'd paused an extra moment, willing him to meet her gaze. He hadn't.

The plane bumped over a particularly large rut in the runway, scattering her papers onto the floor in front of her seat.

"Shit!" *Pay attention to what you're doing,* she scolded herself, waving away Murray's attempts to help her retrieve the documents.

Another lurch. She was starting to wonder if she should be more concerned about getting off the plane, rather than how well she was going to do on her first overseas command.

Major Collins. She savored her new title, but it was her new responsibilities that gave her the most pleasure. As a captain she could have commanded one of the Civil Affairs companies, but time and again she'd watched that honor go to someone else while she was forced to remain at Fort Bragg handling the domestic logistics.

She stared down at the command tree. Matt was part of a four-man platoon under the command of Captain Mark Wilkes. Communications, they had said. *Communications my Aunt Fanny!*

Captain Wilkes' bright blue eyes stared back at her, his smile open. He looked like a baby—hardly out of high school. Was this why she had suddenly been promoted to major? What was so special about this group?

"Master Sergeant, what can you tell me about this unit?" Julie's finger tapped the paper. "Psyops or Delta?"

For the first time since they set out on the mission, he smiled at her. For some ridiculous reason she felt a sense of pride, as if her question had pleased him, as if she had passed some sort of test.

"Both, ma'am."

"The psychological part of the mission I can understand, but Delta is counter-terrorism against America. That's not what we're dealing with here."

"No, ma'am. But the training and principles applied by Delta are useful in other types of work. Psyops is using them to develop elite recon units. Each man is responsible for a different area and works solo. This unit has just been recalled from Afghanistan."

"Solo? I've never heard of solo reconnaissance."

Murray's indulgent smile irritated her. It wasn't like he had years of experience on her. The man couldn't be more than thirty. She not only out-ranked him, she had a good eight years on him—at least!

"It's a fairly new development in field work, ma'am," he said. "It works best when you've got a hostile enemy with no clear base or seat of power. You need to get info, but you have to do it by gaining the trust of the locals. You can't have a full platoon riding around the country asking questions. The captain and lieutenants were specifically requested for this mission."

"And the corporal?" Julie glanced at the page. "Corporal Marshall?"

"He'll remain at the base and co-ordinate the team."

"Why wasn't I told this before?" It irked her that the Master Sergeant had key information about the men in her command that she had not received. Why had she been left out of the loop?

He didn't even have the grace to look uncomfortable with her question. "Strictly 'need to know', ma'am. Now you know."

Julie expelled a slow breath. This was going to be a very interesting mission. The command tree showed Matt's unit separated from the rest of Company A, but the chain of command clearly linked back up to her.

She closed her eyes. It was a mistake. She felt Matt's arms encircle her, his body hard, his lips demanding. His musky scent lingered, overwhelming her senses and transporting her back to last night.

She had noticed him at the bar, where she was celebrating with a few girlfriends from her fitness club in the city. Julie didn't live on the base, preferring to spend her free time in Fayetteville, the nearby town. She loved the anonymity that came with her city life. And last night she had been careful to choose a bar that wasn't frequented by military men. In her position, she didn't need that kind of complication.

He hadn't been able to keep his eyes off her. She could feel him staring at her all evening. Normally, she'd have found this uncomfortable, but last night she'd enjoyed the sensation. It made her feel sexy and desirable. Besides, he was gorgeous!

Buoyed by the day's successes—and maybe a little more wine than she was used to drinking—she had approached him. Almost immediately she felt a connection between them. As they talked, she found herself sharing her deepest desires, and some of her fears. She had never before met anyone who seemed to really 'get' her. But he did.

She had never done anything like this before—picked up a man in a bar and taken him back to her apartment. While not totally inexperienced with men, her experience was definitely limited. For years she had dedicated herself to advancing her career, leaving little time for relationships. And in her line of work, relationships were definitely a problem.

He had been gone when she awoke this morning. Her initial disappointment was quelled as she followed the smell of coffee into her kitchen and read the note he had left. *To be continued... M.*

It had seemed romantic at the time; an indication that he would wait for her return. She never dreamed that he'd be coming with her. Damn him! What was he thinking? Did he really expect them to just continue on?

And then the nagging thought that she had been doing her best to keep at bay needled its way in. *He knew who she was. He had been using her.*

She glanced at Murray, but he was ignoring her, poring over his own notes.

Her head was hurting. She needed to focus on the mission—her first field command. She couldn't allow what happened last night to play on her insecurities.

She didn't know much about Beljou, only what

she had read in tourist brochures. The island, in the Caribbean Sea, was bigger than she thought. Bigger and more remote. The capital, Port-au-Paix, was on the north side of the island, and the resorts and tourist areas lined the coast just east of that. The stats said almost five million people lived on Beljou, but the map didn't show much civilization away from the capital. There were sugar plantations still operating in the center of the island, then a range of mountains and a large section to the southwest that looked dark and inhospitable. *Cap-Verte,* she read.

Finally, the Hercules slowed, shuddered, and came to a lumbering stop. Deafening silence was followed by hollers of "Hurray!" and applause. The pilot high-fived his co-pilot, turned to face the cabin and, with a big grin, doffed his cap with a flourish and waved in appreciation.

She inhaled deeply to slow her frantic heart. *This is it.*

"I should say something." She turned to Murray.

"It's customary," he said.

She frowned. Could he be less helpful? He knew this was her first overseas command and it was crucial that she get the respect of these battle-hardened soldiers. She didn't know why he had been made her aide-de-camp; he had little experience with civil affairs missions. The General had told her to trust the wiry soldier; yet, aside from passing on basic information about the mission, Murray was making no effort to assist her. She was desperate to avoid any missteps.

Outside, voices yelled excitedly as the propellers were secured and wooden blocks placed around the wheels. She hadn't much time.

She stepped into the aisle and turned to the sea of faces looking at her with both curiosity and expectation. Of their own volition, her eyes picked out Matt seated about halfway down the cabin. His face was impassive, his body relaxed. Clearly he hadn't found the flight nearly as nerve-racking as she.

Focus!

"We are entering a particularly unstable situation," she began, her voice strong. "Six weeks ago, at the request of the president of Beljou, the Three-Eighty-Six deployed to this island to support the Beljou government forces after an attack from an organized opposition. This rebel force is supported by some factions of the country's military. The rebels were reacting to the president's failure to honor a promise to call democratic elections. The opposition forces collapsed under the Three-Eighty-Six, and now that the immediate threat has passed, our boys are in the process of withdrawing. The president has agreed to hold elections in six months' time. But first, the country needs some stability. That's our job.

"This is a hearts-and-minds exercise, folks. Our mission is called 'Operation Soft Landing' for a reason. In addition to helping the people of Beljou rebuild their country, we need to reinforce the message that America is a friend. This island is of strategic importance to us—and not just for its sunshine and white, sandy beaches."

Julie paused and looked down the cabin. While most of the soldiers knew the particulars of the mission already, it was important they know her take on the situation. She was relieved when she saw heads nodding in agreement.

"Transportation to barracks has been arranged. We'll regroup for a full briefing at thirteen-hundred."

There was a pounding from outside of the plane. The pilot stepped out from behind his seat to raise the long metal handle that secured the door. After a grunt of complaint from both the pilot and the lock, the door swung slowly outward. In an instant, the hot, damp air of the island replaced the dry heat of the aircraft's cabin—Beljou was about to enter its rainy season.

She turned to take her backpack from the metal rack above her head but Murray stopped her.

"I'll get that, Major," he said quietly.

She looked down at him; perhaps he wasn't trying to thwart her efforts after all.

With a nod of thanks, Julie squared her shoulders, brought herself up to her full six-foot height, and stepped through the door, remembering to duck at the last moment.

She paused at the top of the stairs to take in her surroundings. The airport was nothing like she'd been expecting. Rather than arriving in a Third World country, she thought she could be anywhere in the Western world—barring the men armed with automatic weapons who were strategically placed among the aircraft, of course.

No, this isn't America, she scolded herself crossly, *and you'd do well not to forget it!*

She could see several military planes among the grounded commercial aircraft—most bore an American flag. On the ground, an assortment of vehicles shuttled people and cargo. A buzz of voices and laughter, motors idling, and engines revving filled the air. And the colors! Anyone who wasn't wearing military khaki was attired in festive reds, greens, yellows, and oranges. The atmosphere more resembled a carnival than an airport in a country rife with conflict and internal strife.

Julie raised her face to the glorious sun. A few wisps of cloud lingered in a brilliant blue sky, and a gentle breeze carried a light salty flavor. She inhaled deeply, then choked. Diesel fuel, too.

In the distance she could see the outline of a sprawling city surrounded by small, dirty brown hills. The flat roofs of the houses resembled a poorly assembled patchwork quilt. Off to the left she saw a mound shimmering with color and movement. As she looked closer, her heart leapt into her throat. It was a dump. The colors were people pushing through the piles of rubbish and batting away great winged scavengers.

She lowered her gaze to the young private at the bottom of the stairs. He was standing beside a running jeep and looking up at her expectantly.

Well, she thought, forcing the image of the dump and its pitiful occupants from her mind, *no time to dally.*

Julie descended the steps with as much authority as she could muster. Operation Soft Landing was underway.

****

Whew, I'm glad that's over, Julie thought as she stepped into her new office. She had been nervous during her first formal briefing to her troops. After twenty years in the military, it annoyed her that she still questioned her abilities; a legacy from her father, no doubt. But whatever their reasons for overlooking her in the past, she was here now, and she would show her superiors how competent a leader she was.

"Well I have to say, this is a big improvement on a tent in the desert."

She whirled around to see Matt leaning casually against the doorframe. Her knees buckled and she grabbed the edge of a chair. *Damn!* How could a pair of sexy dark eyes have this effect on her? She watched dumbfounded as Matt entered the office and slowly turned, appearing to inspect the room from all angles. It didn't escape her notice that he failed to salute her.

He whistled in appreciation. "It's not often us poor schleps get to live in a palace. In fact, it's a first for me." He gave her a brilliant smile.

It was true. The facilities were spectacular. The president had retreated to his plantation estate, leaving his palace in the city to the American command. If the mission was extended for any great length of time, the troops would have to be housed elsewhere—finding those lodgings was another item on her 'to do' list. For now, however, they were sleeping under gilt-laden ceilings, eating in grand dining halls, and working in salons that a few months before had entertained dignitaries and celebrities. It was a stark contrast to the slums through which they had driven from the airport.

"What are you doing here?" she said, finally finding her words. As soon as she uttered them she wished she had remained silent; the question sounded stupid.

"Here, as in Beljou? Or here, as in your office?"

"Both." She hated how calm he appeared, as if it was the most natural thing in the world for him to be here.

As his smile broadened, she found herself staring at his lips. She shivered as the memory of that mouth moving delicately along her neck sent tendrils of heat coiling through her belly.

"Well, I'm in Beljou because this is where I've been posted by the powers-that-be. And I'm in your office because I thought you might want to talk. I mean, after last night..."

"You thought *I* wanted to talk?" His words incensed her. What about him? Who did he think he was to condescend to her? "Don't patronize me. I was completely up-front with you. I told you who I was, and what I did. It seems *you* left out a few details, though."

"Look—" He took a step towards her.

She backed away, tripping over the leg of the chair to which she was clinging. In an instant he was beside her, his arm wrapped around her waist, steadying her. She knew she should pull away, but couldn't find the will.

Memories came flooding back, not just the physical sensations—she could deal with those—but also the emotional connection he'd made with her. Last night he had touched something deep within her. He had seemed to see beyond her insecurities and conflicts to the woman she really was. He had made her think that it was possible to be true to herself and her calling, and still be a desirable, sensual woman.

"You are *so* beautiful." His voice was rough.

Julie's breath caught at the delicate brush of fingertips across her temple as he tucked a stray lock of her short blond hair behind her ear. She inhaled his heady masculine scent.

She could see the pulse in his neck beating furiously and wondered if she was causing it. She raised her gaze to his and saw the answer. His already dark eyes were black with a passion that matched her own.

What am I doing? I don't even know who this guy is. She stepped away, desperate to put distance between them.

He sighed heavily.

"Why didn't you tell me you were part of this mission?" Julie asked.

He shrugged. "It didn't really come up. You were obviously on a high from your promotion and new command, and we were celebrating. We didn't really talk about me at all."

She stared at him incredulously. "Surely you knew I was your commanding officer?"

"Well, technically you weren't my C.O. until the start of the mission—which was oh-six-hundred this morning. Last night, you were just... well..." He paused, a sheepish grin playing on his lips.

"Just! I was *just* what?" Anger sizzled through her. Was she just another fling to him? Had she only imagined the connection between them?

"Whoa!" He held up his hands and stepped towards her.

She backed away, panicked. She didn't dare let him touch her again. She couldn't trust her traitorous emotions.

He stopped, dragged in a deep breath and began again. "Last night you were *just* a beautiful, sexy, engaging woman that I wanted to spend time with."

Julie stared at him. Her tension melted away, replaced by a tangible need. God, he was gorgeous! At well over six feet he made her feel almost petite—an unusual experience. His broad shoulders tapered to a slim waist, enhanced by the tight green T-shirt tucked into his camouflage pants. His jet-black hair was close-cropped, but not as short as the current military fashion. She could remember the silky feel of it through her fingers as she had clung to his kisses and pulled him closer. His face had the chiseled features of his Native American heritage and gave him an exotic look. And those onyx eyes: as deep and dark as a bottomless pool. She had seen them burn with passion last night, and then, again, a few moments ago.

Was he playing with her? Why had he let things go as far as they had? He knew who she was *now*.

"It should never have happened." She tried to sound calm and reasonable.

"I didn't lie to you."

"That's not the point. The omission is a lie. You know fraternization is against regs. We could both get court-martialed over this."

She drew herself up to her full height and glared at him.

He looked down and seemed to be considering his options. Then he raised his head and shrugged his shoulders. "I'm sorry, Major. I have no explanation for my behavior."

His response stunned her. But it was the way her heart tumbled in her chest at his far away, almost regretful look that surprised—and dismayed—her most. *Don't give in.*

"I want it clearly understood that what happened is in the past. It was what it was, but it's over." She took a deep breath and hardened her resolve. She couldn't let him get to her. "From this point forward, I am your C.O. and that's all. We have a job to do and I'm here to see that it gets done. Consider this a verbal warning, Lieutenant. I expect you to remain squeaky-clean for the duration of the mission."

She immediately regretted the harsh words; an official warning was a bit extreme. But he'd shaken her world and made her question herself at a time when she couldn't afford to do so. And like a wounded animal, she lashed out at the cause of her pain.

"Are you sure that's what you want?" he seemed skeptical. "Can you forget so easily?"

She wavered only briefly. Now was not the time to be second-guessing her decisions. She needed to secure her command, and earn the respect of her soldiers. Until she was able to ensure her emotions were under control, the more distance she put between Matthew Wolf and herself the better.

"Yes, sex can be a powerful force, but like other physical wants it can be controlled."

"What's between us is more than sex." His voice had become husky. "Although, I have to say, that part was pretty fantastic."

Julie hated the immediate flush that overwhelmed her body as memories of their lovemaking flooded her senses. *Blast him!*

"I think you have an exaggerated sense of yourself. How on earth could there be anything more than a physical attraction between us when we only spent a few hours together? And you didn't even have the decency to be honest about who you really were." She could taste the bitterness of her words, but was helpless to soften their effect. "There is nothing 'to be continued'."

She saw a flash of anger—or was it hurt?—in his eyes.

"That's it? You think we can just start over as if nothing happened?"

"What more do you want, Lieutenant?" She forced herself to look directly into his eyes.

He stared back for a long moment, then dropped his gaze and snapped to attention.

"Nothing, ma'am."

"Good. Dismissed."

He turned on his heel and strode toward the door. He paused on the threshold and she feared he was going to turn and say something. *Just go!* She couldn't bear any more. Then he seemed to change his mind. He squared his shoulders and marched out the door, in what she was sure was an exaggerated manner.

She sank down onto the chair and laid her head on her desk, exhausted. She could feel tears welling in her eyes, but she forced them back. How could this be happening to her? How could one man, no matter how good looking or how great a lover, have this effect on her?

Get a grip, Jules! You've worked far too hard to blow it for some GI Joe who looks hot in a tight tee.

Despite her resolve, Julie knew in her heart that it was more than just amazing sex that drew her to Matthew Wolf. He had allowed her a glimpse of what her life could be like with *all* her dreams fulfilled.

Alone, in the empty office, an overwhelming sense of loss washed over her.

****

"That went well," Matt said sarcastically under his breath, as he strode down the hallway away from Julie's office.

He shook his head in frustration. He wished he had a more satisfactory explanation for his behavior the night before. Wasn't it enough that they were attracted to one another? More than attracted. There had been a lot more going on than just the physical; they had definitely connected on a whole other level. But jeez, it had only been one night—a few hours even.

She was taking this far too seriously. What difference did it make that in the morning she'd be his C.O.? Well, okay, if he was honest with himself, he had to acknowledge it would have made a difference. Otherwise, he would have told her who he was. But he didn't, and they had had a fantastic time. And it's not like their night together made any difference to the mission.

It was unsettling, though, to have a woman like her think beyond simply bedding him. This had to be a first.

He glanced at his watch. Only forty-five minutes until he needed to report to get his assignment. Right now he needed to find somewhere to be alone to collect his thoughts and figure out how he was going to get through this mission. He could just slip into one of the alcoves off the corridor—he remembered seeing one just a little way along.

Ahead, one of the palace staff was coming towards him. He'd rather avoid anyone while he was in this black mood. He looked around for an alternate corridor. When he turned back, the man had gone. Intrigued, Matt continued along the hallway searching for doorways or other exits that the man had escaped through. He found none. It was as if the man had vanished into thin air.

Although his curiosity was piqued, Matt had more important things to worry about at the moment. He slipped into the alcove, leaned heavily against the wall, and tried to silence his mind.

He knew which area he'd request to be assigned to. And he'd get it, too. No one else was particularly interested in being too far from the base. He, on the other hand, couldn't wait to get away from the bureaucracy of command—the farther the better. And this time, it had the added bonus of also complying with his C.O.'s wishes. Cap-Verte was pretty much as far away from Port-au-Paix—and from Julie—as he could get. Maybe that would give him bonus marks with the senior command. God knows nothing else had worked.

He was excellent at his job—his service record proved it. He had earned numerous commendations and awards, not only for service rendered but for bravery, too. Nevertheless, when it came time to look for unit leaders, the senior command consistently passed him over. Time and again, men, younger men, were promoted ahead of him for positions he deserved.

After twenty-two years of disappointment, he should have seen it coming. The quick promotion of Brownwell from Second Lieutenant to First—his equal—had upset, but not surprised him. The final straw had come when Wilkes, a kid, had been made Captain, and tagged to head the unit.

It had been difficult to sit through the briefing at the Pentagon after the promotions had been announced. But to come to Fort Bragg and have to socialize with his unit before shipping out? That was almost too much. He'd needed some time to get his game-face on.

He had known when he suggested it that the jazz club would be too quiet for the younger guys. Wilkes, Brownwell and Marshall had one drink, and then took off for more excitement. Alone at last, Matt contemplated his options.

His four-man unit had been called back from Afghanistan specifically to participate in this mission. They had been told that their commander would be Major Julie Collins—another newly promoted soldier. The Collins family was legendary in military circles. Both generals, her grandfather had distinguished himself in the Second World War, and her father had been named Army Chief of Staff a few years ago. Her two older brothers seemed destined to follow the family tradition. Matt hadn't realized there was a daughter, too. *Poor girl,* he thought. *That family reputation must be quite a cross to bear.*

He had recognized her immediately when she walked into the club. She had the same profile as her brother—Matt had served under Richard Collins as part of the NATO forces in Serbia—but there was nothing masculine about her. The gentle slope of her cheek flowed gracefully down to her jaw and then onto a long, elegant neck. Her lips were full and inviting, animating her face when she smiled.

He hadn't realized he'd been staring until she turned and their eyes locked. Deep blue, they took his breath away. She cocked her head to the side, a slight smile played on her lips. When she turned away, he gasped as the smoke and liquor-infused air rushed back into his lungs.

Blonde-hair, blue-eyes is not for you, Boyo, the familiar admonishment repeated. *As if.*

But then she was standing in front of him. And then she sat down and began talking to him. And then he forgot about wanting to be alone.

He offered to walk her home. She accepted. Her long fingers wrapped easily around his broad hand. He knew they made a striking couple. Both tall and slim, her golden beauty was a stunning contrast to his dark features.

Blonde-hair, blue-eyes is not for you, Boyo.

Shut up!

It was cold outside, and he slipped his arm around her so they could share each other's warmth. He kissed her at her door. Her response was tentative at first, but within seconds, he could feel a rising fire of passion in her that matched his own growing need. The tension that had seized him all evening exploded in a kaleidoscope of sensations as he felt her melt into him...

A shrill screech knifed into his consciousness.

Where am I? His heart pounded wildly as he struggled to slow his breathing and re-orient himself in the palace alcove. He could still feel the aching need...

Then he heard it again; a high-pitched scream. And it was coming from the direction of Julie's office.

CHAPTER 2

Julie's head snapped up and, in one fluid movement, she rose from her chair and unsheathed her Browning nine-millimeter pistol, a present from her father. Her eyes scanned the room and she slowly approached the door—the direction from which the scream had come.

Just outside her office, a young girl stood immobilized in terror, hands at her face, her eyes wide. Then she screamed again.

Julie looked around, but could see no one. Her heart slowed to a normal beat as she slid the safety lock into place and holstered her gun.

Holding both hands up to show the girl she had nothing to fear, she tried to calm her.

"Il est bien. Vous êtes sauf. Personne vais vous blaissez." It's okay. You're safe. No one's going to hurt you, she said awkwardly in French, knowing it was the language spoken on the island.

The girl looked at her, confusion plainly evident on her face. The moment quickly passed, and she launched into a stream of verbiage that Julie couldn't understand.

She looked closer at the girl. She wore a pink jumper over a white blouse—it reminded Julie of a school uniform—and her feet were bare except for loose sandals. She was older than Julie had first thought—a young woman really. Her hair was tied back tightly and it seemed to be brown and smooth, not the kinky black hair of the Beljouans of African decent. Her complexion was dark but her eyes were... blue?

Footsteps pounded closer, and Julie turned to see Matt racing towards her, his firearm drawn. She held up her hand to slow his advance.

"It's okay. I'm just trying to calm her down. I don't know what she's afraid of."

"Oh."

She looked at him in surprise. He couldn't possibly have thought *she* was the one who had screamed, could he? From the look on his face, that was exactly what he had thought.

She wasn't sure if she was touched or annoyed by his assumption. Her heart fluttered as his eyes betrayed a level of concern beyond that of a soldier for his C.O. But she was his C.O. and hadn't risen to the rank of Major without considerable experience in handling potentially dangerous situations.

Her head began to hurt. Things were so complicated when Matt was around.

She turned her attention back to the woman and tried again. "*Comment vous appellez-vous?*" *What's your name?*

Again, the woman began to speak rapidly in a language that sounded somewhat French, but was impossible for Julie to make out.

Behind her, she sensed Matt jump to attention and silently cursed her body for its heightened awareness of his presence.

She looked up to see an officer approaching. Although he walked quickly, he didn't seem to be rushing. A cap covered his close-cropped hair, but she could tell from the stubble on his face that he was a redhead.

He stopped, took in the scene and turned towards Julie, ignoring Matt.

"*Major* Collins," he said, with a wide grin that split his freckled face.

The emphasis on her rank was deliberate, Julie thought. His warm hazel eyes seemed to wrap her in a blanket of calm, and she forgave him his pretension.

"I am Colonel Bernard Sinclair. Please forgive me for not meeting you when you arrived. Another pressing matter unavoidably detained me. I hope my aide was agreeable and got you properly settled in."

He was from the South, judging by how he drew out the syllables of his words. *But where?* As an Army brat, she had lived on military bases all over the country. She and her brothers used to entertain themselves by guessing where people were from based on their speech patterns. Julie was the acknowledged champion.

"Thank you, Colonel. Everything was just fine."

"And what is going on here, may I ask? I thought I heard a scream a moment ago."

Louisiana! she thought in triumph, and suppressed a smile.

"I don't know what's wrong. I've tried to talk to her. She seems to understand what I'm saying, but I can't make out what *she's* saying."

"I suspect your formal French is too refined for the *patois* spoken by the locals here," he said as though he was a host apologizing for some inadequacy in his hospitality. "I'm from New Orleans. I think our Creole may be a little closer. Do you mind if I try?"

"Please."

She listened with fascination as Colonel Sinclair and the woman spoke with both words and broad arm gestures. She could pick out an occasional word or phrase, although not enough to fully follow their conversation.

As they spoke, the woman grew calmer. Finally, he patted her on the shoulder and she turned, curtsied to Julie and ran off down the hallway, her sandaled feet slapping a tattoo on the marble floor.

"Poor girl. Absolutely terrified. She doesn't know

anything, though. Was just coming down the hall, to your office, Major, when she saw this." He pointed to the floor.

Julie looked down. At her feet was a strange pattern. It looked like a crude picture of a cloud with rain and two lightning bolts coming from the sky.

Where did that come from? It hadn't been there when she entered her office forty-or-so minutes ago. In the confusion brought on by the woman's screams and their language difficulties, she hadn't noticed it until now.

"So, Lieutenant... Wolf," Colonel Sinclair said, angling his head to read the name on Matt's uniform. "What's your read?"

Matt was squatting on the floor, a pad and pen in hand copying the pattern. "I was going to ask you, sir." He glanced up briefly and then resumed his copying. "Have you seen anything like this before?"

The Colonel walked around the drawing, stopping behind Matt to examine his reproduction. "I can't say as I have. Neither here nor in New Orleans. What about you, Lieutenant? I believe there are certain similarities between the indigenous Indians of Beljou and our own Native Americans?"

"No, sir, I've never seen anything like it." Matt closed his pad and stood up.

"We've had a few incidents with the boys playing around with the local legends. You know, trying to spook each other," Sinclair continued. "In fact, that's what held me up earlier today. It seems one of our corporals was convinced by one of the boys that his, ah..." he glanced at Julie, "dalliance with a local girl had gotten the attention of the mambo, and she had put a hex on him. We've had some dolls turn up, too. But nothing like this."

Julie stared at the two men. What were they talking about?

They must have seen her confusion because they

both smiled and said at the same time, "Voodoo," and then laughed together.

"You're joking," she said, unreasonably annoyed at their camaraderie.

"Oh, no," Colonel Sinclair responded. "Voodoo's a big part of the culture here."

"There are a lot of myths about what voodoo really is," Matt said. "All the hype around Mardi Gras and stories about New Orleans haven't helped—no offense, Colonel."

"None taken." He turned to Julie. "The Lieutenant's correct. New Orleans has a whole industry built around voodoo legends. But what most people think of as voodoo bears little resemblance to reality.

"Voodoo combines the beliefs of the indigenous island people with the animal spirit beliefs brought over by the African slaves in the 1700s," Colonel Sinclair continued. "And then just to make things really interesting, bits of Roman Catholic liturgy were picked up from the missionaries and French plantation owners."

"I've heard the stories of voodoo, of course, but I thought it was all made up for the benefit of the tourists. I had no idea voodoo was real. People here practice it? As a religion?" Julie asked.

"They say that Beljou is eighty per cent Roman Catholic and one hundred per cent voodoo," Matt replied.

Colonel Sinclair nodded. "I'd like to think that this particular drawing was left here as a good omen, but I tend to be a suspicious man. It's safer that way."

Julie looked more closely at the picture, now intrigued by its implication. Whatever had been used to make it reminded her of blood. "That's not..."

"Blood?" Matt said, picking up on her train of thought. "Definitely. But not human."

Julie looked skeptical. *How can he know if it's*

human or not?

"The smell," he said, once again appearing to read her mind. "It's from some sort of animal. It's been mixed with something—cornmeal, looks like. The person who did this would have spread it like he was sowing seeds. Given the intricacy of the pattern and the length of time he had to do it, I'd say it was someone who knew what he was doing."

"I agree," Colonel Sinclair said, thoughtfully rubbing the stubble on his chin. "I think we're dealing with something more than just a prank."

"I'll share this with my team and see what we're able to find out-country," Matt said, patting the breast pocket where he had placed his notebook.

"Wouldn't it be better to have a photo?" Julie asked.

"Oh, we'll definitely photograph it," Sinclair said. "And sample the blood, too. But many of the island's inhabitants are funny about photos. It'll be much easier for the Lieutenant and his unit to show a sketch."

Matt nodded thoughtfully, saluted, "Afternoon, Colonel... Major," and walked away.

"So that's Lieutenant Wolf." Colonel Sinclair seemed to be speaking to himself. "I have to admit I was curious, but he seems satisfactory."

"You know Lieutenant Wolf?" Julie was startled.

"Know him? No. Of him? Yes. He has quite the reputation."

Julie was torn. She wanted to know everything the Colonel knew about Matt, but it wasn't solely for professional reasons, and she didn't want to give herself away by appearing too eager for information.

"Is there anything I should know, Colonel?"

"Well," he paused looking uncomfortable. "Lieutenant Wolf has a reputation as a crack communications specialist—exceptional, really. In Afghanistan, he was able to penetrate cells and gain the trust of locals like no one else. But his methods are... ah... unorthodox, shall we say?"

"Unorthodox?

"I'm sure it's all in his file," he said, closing the discussion.

"Probably." Julie wondered how long it would take for the file to arrive from Washington *if* she actually requested it. Just in time for her to read it on the plane home, no doubt. "Thank you for your candor, Colonel."

"Any time, Major. It is a pleasure to serve with you." His smile seeped genuine Southern charm and he gave her a small bow. "I am from a career family, too."

Damn! Her family again.

Promising to send a photographer, and someone to clean the floor, he sauntered away. Then suddenly, halfway down the corridor he stopped.

"I almost forgot," he called back over his shoulder. "We have a C.O.'s breakfast every morning at oh-seven-hundred. I'll see you then."

****

The days quickly settled into a predictable pattern. Julie rose early, took a run around the compound and then did a few laps in the palace pool. Although still early spring, it was getting noticeably warmer and early morning was really the only time physical activity was comfortable. Following a quick shower, she would head to a small dining salon to have breakfast with Colonel Sinclair and the senior Beljou officer assigned to the Americans, Colonel Jean-Marc Gaudet. A meeting with Murray preceded a daily briefing with her troops at oh-eight-hundred hours. The remainder of the day was spent strategizing with her unit heads, digesting reports, and liaising with the locals in and around the compound. Her first days were full and satisfying, but the nights were a different matter entirely.

Julie hadn't seen Matt since the day of their arrival. He had immediately headed into the Beljou countryside to begin the important process of securing reliable sources of intelligence. Each of the men in his unit had been assigned an area to cover. In order to remain close to the command center, the unit's leader, Wilkes, had assigned himself to Port-au-Paix. Matt, she learned, had requested and been given the farthest assignment, in Cap-Verte. She couldn't help wondering if his desire for the remote location had something to do with the "unorthodox methods" Colonel Sinclair had referred to.

While he might not be present physically, she found it difficult to stop thinking about him, especially at night when she fell into bed, exhausted. It was then that the strict control she exerted over her thoughts during the day left her. Try as she did to fight off the dreams that haunted her sleep, each time she closed her eyes, his face loomed in her consciousness and she could, again, feel his hands caressing her skin.

Just at the moment of waking, she would experience the glow of a woman well-loved, but the sensation would be replaced by frustration and anger as soon as she fully awoke.

He had used her. Even if he hadn't asked for anything yet, he would. They all did eventually. He knew that she was his C.O. He knew who her father was. He was ambitious; you didn't volunteer for the most difficult assignments if you weren't.

And yet, that didn't seem like the man she had met in Fayetteville. He had seemed so honorable. He had been caring and thoughtful. She had been so hopeful...

And he had lied—if not outright, then at least by omission. Did she really know him? And what did Colonel Sinclair's comment about unorthodox methods mean? In his role, the ability to lie—and seduce women—would be an asset. Was that it?

She did her best to convince herself that her dreams were a response to the inner loneliness she was feeling. As the C.O., she wasn't in a position to socialize with her troops. Sometimes in the evening she would walk past the mess hall and hear the raucous laughter of the men and women—her own troops as well as the remaining members of the Three-Eighty-Six—as they played cards and tried to one-up each other with their war stories.

The other C.O.s were certainly friendly enough, but it was clear that she was the junior member of the team—and a woman.

It was ironic that the person she felt closest to was Murray. The cunning little man was proving to be just as reliable as the General had promised. Easily accepted where she couldn't go, he had become her eyes and ears within her troops.

Despite his relative youth, Murray had seen more action than many other soldiers. Julie sometimes wondered if he resented being pulled from a combat posting to participate in this reconstruction and restoration mission. If so, he never gave any hint of it.

Julie spent most of her time with Suzanne, the young woman who had been so traumatized by the drawing on the floor outside of her office that first day. She had been assigned as an assistant, of sorts. It was her responsibility to ensure that Julie was fed and had adequate supplies. She also cleaned the office and did laundry.

Julie tried several times to ask Suzanne about the drawing, but found the girl unhelpful. An orphan of mixed European and African descent, she'd been raised by Catholic nuns and taught to fear the traditional voodoo culture of the island. While she lacked knowledge of modern-day Beljou, she held a wealth of information about the history of her own mixed heritage.

Unlike their American counterparts where they inherited slave status if the mother was a slave, mulattos in Beljou were often highly educated and wealthy, and in the past had even been slaveholders. Not entirely welcome in either the French or African cultures, many had been slaughtered and now made up only a tiny minority of the country's population. Nevertheless, Suzanne carried her mixed heritage with pride, often deriding the cultures of the French colonists *and* the African slaves they'd imported.

Julie learned all this during her daily Beljou-Creole lessons with Suzanne. The young woman took great delight in correcting Julie's word choices and laughed uproariously at her pronunciations.

Unencumbered by the restrictions of military hierarchy, Julie found Suzanne's company refreshing and often took her along when she ventured into Port-au-Paix. Suzanne was as unfamiliar with her surroundings as Julie was, so together they explored the city.

Julie was very careful when they went out. She knew from the reports she had received which areas of the city were relatively safe and which to avoid. Despite the outward appearance of calm, Port-au-Paix and its inhabitants sizzled with an undercurrent of tension that was ready to erupt at any moment.

Returning from one of these sojourns, she spotted Master Sergeant Murray hurrying towards her from across the compound. Usually composed, she was surprised by his obvious agitation.

"The General's on the phone for you, ma'am. It's the third time he's called this afternoon."

Ah, that explains it.

She thanked Murray, told Suzanne she wouldn't need her any more that day, and leisurely made her way to her office.

"General?"

The phone line crackled, and Julie felt his

annoyance even before he spoke.

"Is that any way to address your father?"

She closed her eyes, took a deep breath and counted to three. Damn him! Why couldn't she ever do anything right in his eyes? Every time they spoke he made her feel like a naughty child.

"Well, considering this is a secure, *military* phone line, I assumed this was an official call."

"It is an official call, but you don't have to be so damned formal. Whether you like it or not, you *are* my daughter. A few niceties wouldn't kill you."

She was on thin ice. She wasn't a child anymore and, father or not, he was the Army Chief of Staff. At the very least, the position demanded her respect.

"Yes, sir. I'm sorry."

"I've read the official reports and everything seems to be going well. But I want to know how *you* are finding your new command. How's it going?"

Checking up on me? "Everything is great. You were right about Murray. He's a godsend."

Thankfully, their strained conversation was brief. Julie slumped into her chair as she hung up the phone and willed away the threatening tears.

After all these years he still saw her as the rebellious teenager who defied him at every opportunity. How many other C.O.s did he personally call? None!

He had never accepted her decision to join the military. She suspected he'd rather she stayed home, married a military man and raised babies, just like her mother.

All she wanted was to make a name for herself—to be successful on her own terms. Both her brothers had been made colonels by the time they were forty. She had heard the rumors that their spectacular rises were the result of their family connections, but Julie knew it wasn't true. They were exceptional officers who had proven themselves and were rewarded for it.

What, then, was wrong with her? While most would consider her military career to be on the fast track, she felt she was nowhere near to matching their success. And until a month ago, she had thought her career was stalled.

The unexpectedness of her promotion and the suddenness of her field command troubled her. Her father's phone call had done nothing to ease her mind. The only thing worse than his daughter joining the military, Julie thought cynically, was his daughter not succeeding in the military. How far would he go to protect the hallowed Collins name?

****

Matt slapped Jimmy on the back, wished him "*Bonswa!*" and then peeled off from the group of Beljouans arriving at the compound to begin their shift. Jimmy, the older black man who oversaw the kitchen staff, had been regaling him with stories of those *soldats maudits*—damn soldiers—and their crazy antics. Jimmy's stories about what was going on in the compound were informative as well as entertaining.

Matt was dressed as a local in loose-fitting pants, a bright turquoise shirt, and a broad-brimmed hat. He wore several multi-colored bracelets around his wrists and a turquoise necklace that had been given to him by Madame Lucie. His uniform was stuffed into the plain backpack he carried, along with his gear. Because of his dress and features the group had assumed he was one of the island's natives. He hadn't bothered to enlighten them.

He probably should have formally checked in at the gate but, frankly, he was too tired for the strict protocol he'd be required to follow. He didn't want to see Captain Wilkes tonight—tomorrow was soon enough. And he sure didn't want to see Julie—at all. He wouldn't be back here if his radio hadn't conked out—the humidity was wreaking havoc with the batteries. Such a change from the desert of Afghanistan!

He breathed in deeply, welcoming the cool night air.

The light from the full moon was like a spotlight on the elaborate walkways that meandered through the grounds, but he kept to the shadows of the palace. While the fountains had been turned off, he noticed that the gardens were still being maintained.

He'd seen a lot in his travels, but it always came down to the same issue—innocent people, just trying to get through life, caught up in the powerful ambitions of a few men: families torn apart by politics and the aspirations of petty warlords; women and children killed—or worse. And then the West rides in with their white hats and their big guns to save the day. Did they help? Sometimes. But at what cost?

Careful, Boyo. You're one of the cowboys, remember?

As he rounded a corner, lost in his familiar inner debate, he saw Julie and stopped dead.

She was sitting alone on a bench under an enormous tree; her head tilted back, her eyes closed. The moon shone down on her through the leaves and her beauty again struck Matt, even as he cursed the effect she had on him.

You'd better get your act together, Boyo. This is going nowhere.

He gave himself a mental shake. She'd made her position perfectly clear. And hadn't he had enough experience with her type to know that she meant it?

Now, as he looked at Julie, the mental anguish he'd managed to keep at bay for the last few weeks was growing to a physical ache in his chest. She had made him forget his loneliness—for a night. That was why he felt this emotional connection to her. He would allow her that. But anything more? No way!

She didn't see him standing in the shadow. He

could just skirt around her to get to the barracks. She'd never know he'd been here. Except that he realized he was walking straight towards her. *OH-tuh*! His mother's curse came quickly to his mind.

Her eyes fluttered opened as he stepped out of the shadows, and widened with surprise as she recognized him. She leapt to her feet.

"Ma—Lieutenant Wolf?"

"Major." Without thinking he removed his hat.

"What are you wearing?"

He looked down at his clothes and shrugged.

She shook her head. "You look like a local."

"That's the idea."

"Well, you've done a good job of it. But how does that reinforce the message that we're bringing safety and goodwill to the island? America, I mean."

All business. He sighed.

"I only wear this when I need to make myself invisible. Most of the time I'm in uniform."

"And you need to make yourself invisible here because...?"

Busted!

"Found any more voodoo drawings?" he asked, hoping to change the subject.

The diversion worked. She gave him a suspicious look but didn't press him for an answer.

"No. Have you been able to find out anything about them?"

"A bit. They're *vèvès* and they're meant to represent the island's voodoo spirits—*lwas,* they're called. Each *lwa* has its own *vèvè* design—yours by the way is Oya, a warrior death goddess." He paused, wondering if he should tell her the rest. She should know, he decided. "She's also known as the one who puts on pants to go to war."

Julie looked visibly startled.

"Well, that settles it, doesn't it?" she said matter-of-factly. "It obviously *was* meant for me. But why?"

Matt admired her spunk. It had to be intimidating to arrive at your first overseas command and immediately be confronted by what was potentially a voodoo curse. He wondered how she had been managing these first few weeks, and wished he didn't care.

"I don't know what it means. *Vèvès* are used to invoke the spirits, and the locals make sacrifices and offerings to them. But this particular one? I just haven't been able to find out anything specific—yet."

"I see." She nodded pensively. "And the rest of your mission? I know you'll be providing a full report to Captain Wilkes, but how about the highlights?"

"Good," he paused. "Very good." For some reason he was reluctant to talk to her about what he had seen—the poverty and misery he had encountered. Yet despite these things, these were a people with an incredible ability to rise above their wretchedness. The island was rife with violence, but then its history was a violent one. It was unreasonable, he knew, but tonight, in these glorious gardens illuminated by the light of the moon, he desperately wanted to shield Julie from the ugliness beyond the palace walls.

It was suddenly very important to him that she look out for her own safety.

"Look, I don't know if the *vèvè* we found is a good omen or a bad one. It all depends on the intent of the artist. Just be careful."

"Do you think I'm in danger?"

She looked up at him, vulnerable in the moonlight—her eyes wide and trusting. *OH-tuh!*

He took a step closer to her. He could feel her quick breaths on his cheek. His hand began to rise to stroke her face. He wanted to take her in his arms and still the quiver of her bottom lip.

With incredible self-control he stopped himself and took a step back. He wouldn't make the same mistake again.

"I don't know. But someone in this compound drew that picture and until we know why... just be careful."

As he turned and walked away, he could have sworn he heard a sigh of regret. But he couldn't be sure which of them had made it.

CHAPTER 3

The sound of voices wafted out from the briefing room. Julie stopped just outside the door, a smile on her lips. These were her troops and she was proud of what they'd been able to accomplish in just a few weeks. The self-doubts she'd been battling after the General's telephone call had disappeared, replaced by a confidence in her ability to make the right choices in both her career and personal life.

It's amazing what a brisk morning swim after a good night's sleep can do for you.

She had been surprised by how easily sleep had found her last night. Her mind had been spinning when Matt left, and her body... well, best not to think about what her body had wanted.

At least her dreams of Matt had kept thoughts of her father far enough at bay for her to come to her senses. The General was by-the-book and she was sure he wouldn't interfere with the normal course of her career. He didn't want her in the military, anyway. If he was going to use his influence, he'd be more likely to try to thwart her career aspirations. Still...

"Major?"

She started. Murray was standing at the door.

"Everyone's assembled, Major. Are you ready?"

"Yes, thank you, Master Sergeant."

Julie squared her shoulders and followed him into the room. At the podium, she looked up from her notes and directly into a pair of dark, sexy eyes. Her breath caught in her throat and she momentarily lost her train of thought.

Get a grip, Jules. You knew he was here.

The reality of seeing Matt in the flesh so soon after dreaming about being with him bodily was almost too much to endure. She felt faint.

Focus! Focus! "Welcome back, Lieutenant Wolf. Nice of you to join us." *Good recovery, Jules.*

"It's a pleasure to be with you, ma'am," he responded, the corners of his mouth twitching slightly.

Damn! He had seen her reaction to him. Well, nothing she could do about it now. Just get on with the briefing and hope that no one else had noticed her discomfort.

"I have some general notes but, perhaps, Lieutenant Wolf, you can update us on your findings first."

"I'd be happy to, Major."

Matt walked to the front of the room and stepped up onto the tiny dais beside Julie. The heat of him warmed her arm and she quickly stepped down. Now, on the floor, she was forced to look up at him, and she didn't like that sensation, either.

"Like the rest of the country, the southern mountain region is a place of extreme poverty," he began. "The people—mostly the women, but also the elderly—work from dawn to late into the night, just to get enough food to put on the table for the children. If the men haven't joined the revolution on one side or the other, they've been killed; or they're hiding in the mountains and are of no help to their families.

"Our presence here is viewed with extreme ambivalence by the villagers. So, the bottom line, as far as I can tell, is the villagers won't interfere with what we're doing so long as we don't jeopardize their families. But we can't rely on them for help, either. As for the men: whether they are bandits, revolutionaries, or simply desperate, they're very dangerous because their loyalties cannot easily be determined."

Julie was only half listening. She had reviewed Matt's report to Wilkes earlier and shared his findings with the other C.O.s at their breakfast briefing. Instead, she was willing her body to be still while she attempted to regulate her breathing.

Her gaze traveled down the length of the room. It was enormous; far too large for the purpose to which it had been assigned. Her company, requiring only about half of the space, had pulled forward an assortment of chaise lounges, over-stuffed chairs and side tables, leaving the back part of the room devoid of furniture. Artwork from the front of the room had been removed from the walls and stacked neatly to make space for an assortment of topographical maps and flip charts. Those paintings that remained, displayed the bright colors Beljouans loved. But these were not the fun, friendly scenes of everyday life she'd seen for sale in the markets; these were heavily religious, depicting black Jesuses on crosses, and martyrs meeting their various ends. Large intricately patterned golden frames—probably real gold—surrounded each picture.

"Of most concern is a charismatic leader known as the Hougan," Matt was continuing. "While his official line is that he wants to bring back the old ways, he seems to be just another bandit looking for easy riches. He's telling the villagers what they want to hear, and many see him as the salvation of their homes and heritage.

"Right now his support is limited to a few villages, but it seems to be growing, especially in Cap-Verte, across the southern mountains. The supporters he has are zealots, totally committed to him. They are well-organized and well-armed. Their activities, to date, have focused on extorting money from wealthy plantation owners and kidnapping foreigners for ransom.

"Despite its isolation from the rest of the island, Cap-Verte is responsible for a disproportionately high number of Beljou's military rulers, including the current president. It's often seen as the hotbed of discontent for the country. The people are poor, mainly the descendants of slaves who escaped the plantations by hiding deep in the forest. The rocky shoreline makes its beaches unattractive to tourists and so the region hasn't received the same economic benefits as the rest of the country. Cap-Verte is cut off, not only physically by the mountains but economically, socially and culturally. Take all the problems you see in the rest of Beljou, multiply them tenfold, and you've got Cap-Verte."

She frowned at Matt's editorializing of the situation. Before she could censor him, he nodded to her, signaling the end of his report and returned to his seat. She continued with the briefing, dismissing the troops twenty minutes later.

"Hey, Wolf, I bet there's a good story that goes along with that jewelry you're wearing." One of the men elbowed Matt as they made their way to the door.

Although Matt now wore his military uniform, he had kept the colored bracelets and turquoise necklace from the night before.

Julie kept her eyes staring straight ahead and tried to ignore the conversation of the men as they filed past her.

"Yeah, remember that honey in Kigali? She gave you a necklace, too."

She recognized Lieutenant Brownwell's voice.

"Yeah, a necklace and a bit more, eh Wolf?" Another voice.

She couldn't hear Matt's response, but stiffened as his laughter joined in with the others as they headed down the hallway.

Well, what did you expect? she thought crossly. Hadn't Colonel Sinclair told her his tactics were questionable? Didn't this prove what she had suspected?

She raised a hand to her face, remembering the concern he had shown for her last night. It was hard for her to believe he would use women for his own ends.

What are you thinking? It's his job to get information. Everyone knows that typically the women know more about what's going on than men in most situations.

But the women will defend their men, and their families—to the death.

Yes, but if you're able to penetrate their guard and get them to trust you, they'll be your best ally. Do you doubt Matt's ability to gain a woman's trust?

No.

Everyone says he's one of the best. Do you begrudge him his methods?

Yes! It's wrong. It's immoral.

Is it? It's life and death for our troops. Is it the morality that bothers you or is it something more? Jealousy?

"Stop it!" She gasped and quickly looked around. The room was empty. *Stop it,* she repeated, to herself this time.

****

Julie spent the rest of the morning reading through logistics reports—or at least trying to. Hadn't she just read that paragraph? Two or three times? She needed some fresh air.

There was a commotion just outside her office and she could hear Suzanne assume an imperial tone with someone. Then she recognized the other voice.

Oh, for the love of... Julie marched into the corridor to try to stave off the latest battle between

Suzanne and Jimmy. It was obvious that Suzanne felt her mulatto heritage made her superior to the African descendant. But the older man had spent many years in the service of the president and risen to the rank of kitchen-master. Regardless of what Suzanne thought, among the palace staff Jimmy ruled supreme.

Julie's stomach rumbled as the heady smell of a meat, combined with fried plantain and tropical fruit, filled the corridor. She didn't have time for this nonsense. She was hungry.

"Thank you, Jimmy. Please put the tray in my office."

With a toss of his head, the man brushed past Suzanne, and laid the tray on a large table by the window. He turned to Julie, bowed, "*Bon appétit,*" and left, but not before thrusting his face very close to Suzanne's and scowling fiercely at her.

"Really, Suzanne, what's the big deal? Just let him bring the tray in," Julie said. Then she noticed the girl hadn't moved and there were tears in her eyes. On impulse, Julie asked her to join her for lunch.

"Oh no, Madame," Suzanne demurred.

But Julie insisted—there was always too much food for her—and Suzanne gave in gracefully.

Julie stepped into the corridor to ask Jimmy to bring another place setting, but he had disappeared. She looked up and down the long hallway. He couldn't possibly have gone far in the few seconds since he left, but he was nowhere to be seen. *Long legs, I guess.*

Suzanne, excited by the prospect of lunching with Julie, raced off to the kitchen to get another place setting.

Julie paced her office, waiting for Julie. She was starving, but it would be rude to start eating before the girl returned. She lifted a corner of the lid off the great serving dish, inhaled deeply, and broke into a smile. Jimmy had prepared her favorite dish, *poule Creole* with a *ti malice* sauce made from sour orange and lime juice, peppers, and shallots. Each meal was served with a *viv*, in this case fried green plantain—or *bananes* as Suzanne called them—but at other times it had been sweet potatoes or yams. After a few days of sending back plates of sweet cakes, Jimmy had finally gotten the message and provided Julie with fresh fruit, usually mangoes, for dessert. Now if she could only get him to hold off on the beer...

Suzanne raced into the room. The color had drained from her face, and she seemed barely capable of speech. "Come" and "again" were the only words Julie could make out.

She rose quickly from her chair and allowed the girl to lead her down the hallway and into the salon where she shared breakfast with the other C.O.s. Suzanne stopped in the middle of the room, and pointed soundlessly to the French doors that led to the courtyard. They were open.

She fingered the handle of her Browning, but didn't unsheathe it as she slowly stepped through the French doors. Her body tensed, receptive to any sound or motion, she looked around.

The courtyard was entirely enclosed. The only access to it lay through the salon. It wasn't large, perhaps only twenty feet squared. Her gaze scanned the ivy-covered walls then fell to the stone-tiled floor. She gasped.

"Get Lieutenant Wolf and Master Sergeant Murray," she called to Suzanne. "And tell them to bring a camera."

In the center of the courtyard was another drawing.

This was quite different from the previous one. There didn't seem to be a recognizable image. This *vèvè*, if that's what it was, consisted of a series of criss-crossed lines forming diamond patterns, with stars in the center. From its color and how the lines were drawn it looked like it had been done by the same person, but she couldn't be sure.

"Which *lwa* are you meant for?" she mumbled to herself, trying to relieve some of the tension she was feeling. "And what do you want?"

She was quite certain it wasn't an accident that it had been placed outside the room where the three commanders met each day. But how long had it been there? And what had Suzanne been doing in this room? Why had she gone out onto the courtyard? Was it just coincidence that she had discovered both *vèvès*?

Murray and Suzanne arrived together. With his usual efficiency he immediately began taking photographs of the scene, while Julie began to question Suzanne.

The young woman had calmed down enough to explain that she'd come into the salon to pick up an extra place setting rather than going all the way to the kitchen, which was housed in a separate building at the far end of the palace.

Julie suspected Suzanne's reluctance to go to the kitchen was really the result of her desire to avoid Jimmy.

Suzanne had found the doors to the courtyard open, and she had gone to close them to keep out the heat.

Julie had never seen the courtyard doors open; they certainly hadn't been open at breakfast that morning.

"Where's Lieutenant Wolf?" She was annoyed by his delay.

"Don't know, ma'am." Murray replied, examining a Polaroid that had just finished developing. "He's left the compound."

"Left? But I thought he wasn't heading out until tomorrow."

"Yes, Major, but he's got a day of R-and-R. I guess he decided he wanted a bit more excitement than beating Lieutenant Brownwell at poker."

"When will he be back?"

"I don't know if he will, ma'am. He's taken all his gear."

****

Matt paused to wipe his brow with the sleeve of his shirt. The sun had almost reached its zenith and the temperature and humidity soared, along with the threatening thunderclouds.

He looked again at the instructions and crudely drawn map Jimmy had given him. Go past the shrine to Saint Therese.

What the heck does a shrine to Saint Therese look like?

One shrine looked pretty much like another to Matt, and there were plenty of shrines throughout Beljou—not only in the cities and villages, but they would appear in the middle of nowhere, not even near a road or trail.

Matt wracked his brain to figure out who Saint Therese was, but was at a loss to do so. His mother had tried to raise him as a good Catholic, bless her, but she usually had to work Saturday nights and Sunday mornings—cleaning businesses that were open the rest of the week. Although she'd made arrangements for one of the neighbors to take him to mass, he would somehow manage to forget all about it. When the neighbors came to collect him, he couldn't be found.

Matt smiled, remembering the adventures he'd had while he should have been boning up on his catechisms. In those days, before high school, he and the other neighborhood kids would stealthily stalk wild animals—Mrs. Turner's long-suffering orange cat, Barney—or blast into outer space to save the world from a dangerous alien—again, Barney.

Aha! There it is. The shrine to Saint Therese, clearly labeled. He pocketed Jimmy's directions and felt, again the message Madame Lucie had asked him to deliver to her sister, Sophie.

"You go back to Port-au-Paix, you deliver to Sophie? Yes?" she had said, handing him a folded piece of paper.

Madame Lucie had never been to Port-au-Paix and had no idea of its size. He agreed to her request, but wondered how on earth he would ever find one woman in a city with a population of well over three million people. He told Madame Lucie as much, but she brushed off his concerns. "No worries. You'll find her." It was then that she had tied the necklace around his throat and given him a blessing for success in his journey.

To his great surprise, finding Sophie, or Mama Sophie as she was known, had been remarkably easy. She seemed to hold the same place in certain circles of the capital as Madame Lucie did in Cap-Verte. Both were mambos, voodoo priestesses.

Tapping his pocket, he wondered again about the message. Something in Madame Lucie's manner suggested it was more than a simple letter from home. It wasn't in a sealed envelope, but it never occurred to him to read it.

A bead of sweat rested precipitously on his eyebrow and he paused to wipe it away, and adjust his pack. He was dressed in the same local attire he'd worn the night before. In his pack he carried his uniform and all his gear. Although he intended to return to the compound that night, he felt more comfortable having everything close at hand. Force of habit—one he was regretting at the moment; the clothes, arms and radio were heavy, and the real heat of the day had yet to hit.

You'd think you could find something better to do on your day off. But what the heck? If this secured his acceptance in Cap-Verte, so much the better. Besides, he doubted Brownwell could afford to lose any more money at cards.

Matt rounded a corner and saw a collection of small buildings in the distance. There were about a dozen of them, made of various materials, mostly aluminum or tin, but a few seemed to be plaster with wooden frames. There was almost nothing around them—no trees, no fields, just dirt. It wasn't surprising; it was this way in all the settlements on the outskirts of the capital. The natural resources had been stripped to allow the many thousands of rural villagers who had flocked to Port-au-Paix to eke out whatever livelihoods they could.

As he approached, Matt could hear singing—beautiful female voices raised joyously in song. Everywhere in this country the women sang. Such a change from Afghanistan. No, he reminded himself, the women had sung there, too. But theirs had been low, mournful tunes. Not at all like these lighthearted, optimistic melodies.

He marveled at the resilience of women the world over. While their men slept, drank, played cards and fought, women did the majority of the work. Yet, in spite of these hardships, they maintained a sense of hope, humor and joy. Without women, society would surely collapse. He smiled sadly, reminded of the sacrifices his mother had made for him.

A small boy ran towards him, talking excitedly. He wore only a pair of too-large pants, held up by a piece of rope.

"I'm looking for Mama Sophie," Matt said, reaching into his pocket for some of the hard candy he carried. He generally found chocolate to be the best incentive, but had learned the hard way that chocolate and extreme heat didn't mix. The memory of trying to clean melted chocolate out of his pocket with nothing but water from his canteen still made him chuckle.

The boy didn't seem to mind. Candy was candy. The smile almost broke his face as he grabbed the small package, unwrapped it, stuffed it into his mouth and held out his hand for more.

"Oh, no, young man. Too much sugar is bad for you." He quickly hid the evidence as he eyed a group of seven or so small children charging towards him. "Mama Sophie?"

"I'll take you." The boy took Matt's hand importantly. He batted away the group of children who had now reached them. "*Grandmère*?" he called. "*Grandmère*, we have a visitor."

Several women emerged from the buildings and Matt scanned them to see if he could tell which was Madame Lucie's sister. He couldn't. The women looked at him cautiously and none approached. A few called their children back and tucked them behind their skirts. Matt didn't blame them. They had no way of knowing who—or what—he was.

He couldn't see any men in the village. Well, that wasn't surprising. The healthy ones were probably working or looking for work in the city, and the older ones would likely have returned to their villages in the countryside. This was nothing more than a bedroom community for Port-au-Paix—Beljou's version of suburbia.

The boy led him into the largest of the plaster and wood huts. Matt paused on the threshold to let his eyes adjust to the dimness.

The room wasn't very large. Its walls were bright orange, with accents of turquoise and blue. A long table ran along one wall. It was covered with a plain red cloth and held a large assortment of bottles and jars, two plastic-headed dolls wrapped in colored cloths and adorned with crucifixes, a deck of cards, and what looked like a human skull. On the far wall, a collection of Christian religious drawings—Beljouan style—had been tacked up. Beside them, painted directly on the wall, was a black-and-white drawing of what looked like a man on a horse, holding a snake. Matt couldn't understand the words that had been written beside it.

He heard a groan, and turned his head sharply towards the opposite corner. An enormous black woman had risen to her feet and was making her way towards him, appearing to float on air. He was surprised such a large woman could be so graceful. She wore a royal blue dress, which several decades ago would have been at the height of fashion, and a blood-red scarf wrapped around her head. It was her eyes that held his attention; they were a piercing jet black and looked as if they could see right into his soul. While physically she couldn't be more different, those eyes told him that this was certainly Madame Lucie's sister.

He lowered his head respectfully, almost a bow, and then raised his gaze to look at her.

"Mama Sophie. I am Lieutenant Matthew Wolf, of the American military. I am here to bring you greetings from my country, and also from your sister, Madame Lucie. She asked me to give you this." He reached into his pocket and withdrew the paper.

She eyed the offering suspiciously and spit on the ground before taking it from him. She opened it slowly, her face giving nothing away. After she had read it over several times, she spoke. Her voice was low, masculine.

"Lieutenant Matthew Wolf. Have you read this paper that my sister has entrusted to you to deliver to me?"

"No, Mama. It was not mine to read."

After what was probably only a few seconds of silence but seemed much longer, she thrust the paper toward him. “Read, Lieutenant Matthew Wolf.”

My dear sister, I hope this letter finds you well. Things here are as you would expect them to be. I am sending this letter with a Lieutenant Matthew Wolf. He is a dog and not to be trusted. I throw a hundred curses on him and advise you to do the same. It would be a blessing if he never left Port-au-Paix. I trust you will make the appropriate arrangements.

L.

Matt stared at the message, his mind racing. His sidearm was easily accessible under the loose fitting shirt, but he was certain the woman didn’t pose an immediate threat to him. The letter didn’t instruct Sophie to kill him, just to make arrangements for it. That was a greater danger.

How could he have been so wrong about Madame Lucie and his work in the south? Could any of her information be trusted? Had he jeopardized the mission? In all his years of reconnaissance work, he had never made a blunder like this. He prided himself on his ability to judge people.

Suddenly Mama Sophie let out a deep-throated laugh and hugged Matt close to her enormous bosom.

“My sister makes a big joke, Lieutenant Matthew Wolf. You pass her test.”

“Test?” Matt tried delicately to extricate himself from Mama Sophie. He struggled to catch the breath that had been knocked from him, not only from the shock of the message but the fierceness of the embrace.

“Of course, a test,” Mama Sophie said dismissively. She glided over to the table, picked up two glasses and inspected them. Apparently deciding they were suitable, she opened one of the bottles and poured a generous amount of an amber liquid into each.

Matt took the glass she offered. He was reluctant to drink it. He felt unsettled. What was going on?

"You think I poison you?" Mama Sophie asked and then chuckled softly. She held up her own glass and downed the entire contents in one gulp. "See, Lieutenant Matthew Wolf, no poison."

Matt took a tentative sip. Rum, and pretty good rum, too. She was waiting. Expecting. He downed the liquid in his glass, setting his throat on fire and bringing tears to his eyes.

"Good." Mama Sophie took his glass and proceeded to fill both again.

Maybe it was the rum, but Matt was starting to make sense of what was going on. Madame Lucie had written the message knowing that if he read it, he wouldn't give it to Sophie. He assumed Sophie would now give him something to return to Madame Lucie to show he passed her test and could be trusted. But how had Mama Sophie known?

She was watching him with *those* eyes.

"The necklace," she said.

He started. He knew she couldn't really read his mind. It was a trick of observation and intuition—something Matt himself was usually very good at—but it disturbed him to have it played on him. She was a couple of steps ahead of him. He fingered the turquoise stones at his neck. Of course, it was the necklace.

"Now, Lieutenant Matthew Wolf, I think maybe I know some things you would like me to tell you."

She motioned to a chair and he sank down grateful to be off his feet for a while. She brought the bottle from the table and descended into the chair across from him.

After an hour and several more glasses of rum, Matt rose unsteadily from his seat. Mama Sophie did indeed know many things that would be valuable to the military. He would arrange for Captain Wilkes to make contact with her. He smiled to himself, imagining the health-conscious Mark Wilkes trying to match Mama Sophie drink for drink. Oh, well, that was his problem.

"And now, Mama Sophie, in return for your hospitality, may I provide you and your village with some assistance? I know your men are very busy in the city—" he stifled a laugh at her disgusted snort, "and many things that they would do are left to the women."

He was put to good use for the rest of the afternoon. Some of the houses were in need of small repairs and there were a number of heavy objects that needed to be moved. It didn't take long for the village women to lose their shyness around him. They even began arguing with each other over whose jobs were more important—particularly after he removed his sweat-soaked shirt. Two of the women grabbed the shirt, each trying to get it away from the other so she could wash it. He hoped they didn't rip it. It was the only one he had—except for his uniform, and he was strangely reluctant to put that on.

He knew the effect he had on women, and he'd be lying if he said it didn't stroke his ego to see the young women vying for his attention. While he was sometimes able to use their infatuation to gain information, he would never take it any further than simple flirting. That way lay disaster. He knew better than anyone what an absent father meant for the women and children left behind.

He also knew his reputation among the troops and even cultivated it. That kind of cachet granted him a level of status that enabled him to fit in more easily with the other troops in the field.

Finally, his jobs completed and his shirt freshly

laundered—he had politely declined the offer to wash his pants—he knocked on Mama Sophie's door to say goodbye. She emerged, turning sideways to fit through the opening, and clutched him to her. She hadn't written a message for him to deliver to Madame Lucie.

"Tell my sister, *na wé sa*—we will see a better day," she whispered, as she tied a necklace of colorful plastic beads around his neck.

Matt wondered what the boys would say when he returned with another necklace. Or what Julie would think. He winced at the thought. He had managed not to think about her for most of the day. Why, now, should she come crashing into his consciousness?

He knew she was attracted to him. If he had any doubt before, her discomfort at the briefing that morning confirmed it. As he watched her, he'd allowed his thoughts to return to their night together in Fayetteville. He even allowed himself to wonder what would happen if he pursued her here? He was certain she would give in to him—their attraction for one another was undeniable. The consequences for both their careers, however, would be disastrous—more so for hers than for his.

He didn't have a lot to lose. He was slowly coming to terms with the knowledge that his military career wasn't going anywhere.

So far he'd been lucky. Since joining the special reconnaissance unit, his leaders had allowed him to do what he needed to do, with little interference. Even Wilkes, with his rucksack full of management courses, seemed content to let him take the tougher assignments and work autonomously. Matt could have taken those courses, too—who knows, they may even have advanced his career—but he was too busy getting the job done to be promoted for catering to the whims of the ever-shifting powers-that-be.

For Julie it was different. She was military born and bred. She was going places, and deservedly so. As much as he wanted to strip away that hard-ass exterior and explore the woman beneath, he wouldn't jeopardize her future. Not for his own needs.

Mama Sophie eyed him curiously. He squirmed under those all-seeing eyes! Matt bowed his head in thanks and turned to leave.

Laughing and singing, the women and children accompanied him to the edge of the community. They crowded around him and hugged him as he left. He was happy no one from the base was able to see this; that would really ramp up his reputation as a ladies' man.

He lazily scanned the horizon and then lowered his gaze to the dusty road ahead—and his heart jumped into his throat.

CHAPTER 4

He saw her. Julie saw recognition, then surprise flash across his face. Matt was coming towards her. For a fleeting moment she wished she had followed her first instinct and fled when she saw he was preparing to leave. Then she steeled herself, ready for a confrontation.

"Major?" he stopped too close for comfort. "What are you doing here?"

She considered lying, but no excuse came to mind. *Dammit! I'm not the one with secrets. I'm his C.O. I don't have to explain anything to him.* "I followed you."

His eyebrows rose in surprise. Whatever he'd been expecting, this wasn't it. "Well, it's getting late," he recovered quickly. "We'd better get back to the compound. Thank God you brought a taxi. I wasn't looking forward to a long hike back. My feet are killing me." He began walking quickly toward the jeep that Julie had left a little further up the road.

"Wait a minute!" Julie ran to follow him and then matched his pace. "Is that all you're going to say? Nothing about what you've been up to?"

"Well, if you've been following me, you know what I've been up to," he said. "In any event, we've only a few hours of daylight left and it's not safe on the roads after dusk. So, I suggest we delay the interrogation until we're back at base."

His damnably reasonable tone irritated her.

As they reached the jeep he tossed his pack in the back and went to slide into the driver's seat.

"Hold off, Lieutenant. I'll drive," Julie said, stepping in front of him. She was frantic to exert some kind of control over the situation.

"You're in full uniform, Major. It will be less conspicuous if I drive." Matt didn't wait for a response as he edged her out of the way and took the driver's seat.

Julie bit off an angry retort and stalked around the jeep to the passenger's seat. She took off her helmet and ran her fingers angrily through her hair. *How dare he?*

"Put your helmet back on!" he barked.

She turned on him. She had gone easy on him up to now, but she would not tolerate insubordination.

"Ma'am," he added, his clamped teeth belying the conciliatory addendum. "Please."

"Who the hell do you think you're talking to, Lieutenant?" Julie had had enough.

"Look, with your helmet on and your height, you'll appear to be a man from a distance. We'll attract less attention." Matt's tone was one of resigned patience, as though he was talking to a child. "Try to tuck as much of your hair under the helmet as you can."

"You think I look like a man?"

Matt turned to her and her heart skipped a beat as a wicked smiled formed on his lips and mischief danced in his eyes.

"I did say from a distance—a very *long* distance," he said.

She sat quietly as he cranked the ignition and turned the jeep around.

"Why are you so worried about not attracting attention? This area is safe. You *walked* here by yourself."

"Yeah, but I'm not in uniform and I can blend in with the natives here. The whole country is ambivalent, remember? Ambivalent to us. Ambivalent to each other. Nothing here is as it seems."

"So you're saying we're *not* safe?"

"I'm saying it would be best if we got back to the compound as soon as possible."

"But I am the problem? The risk?"

"Yes, ma'am."

Damn him, anyway. Why does he always make me feel so inadequate?

Still, she couldn't help feeling a little guilty. Her stated reason, to Murray and Jimmy, for following Matt had been to make sure he had the drawing she'd made of the *vèvè* that had been discovered. Copies had already been given to Wilkes and Brownwell, and she knew her story was just a pretext. She'd really been curious—more than curious—to know where he was going and who he was with.

It appeared that Matt wasn't the cad she had imagined him to be. Rather than finding him in the arms of one of the local village girls, he had, instead, been laboring for them. She sighed as the image of him, shirtless, hammering nails into rusty tin walls, and later, playing with the village children, revived the physical reaction she had to watching him. He had looked so relaxed and carefree, not the restrained, distant man she saw back at base.

For the first time since they'd arrived, she saw traces of the man she'd met stateside. It would have hurt less if someone had actually hit her in the stomach instead of the gut-wrenching pain she felt with the realization of how much she wanted to see *that* man again.

The heat from him, so close beside her, flushed through her body and she shifted restlessly in her seat. A purely physical reaction to a very handsome, virile man, she told herself sharply. Perhaps her body was simply remembering their tryst—the night he had seemed so attentive; *the night he had lied about who he was and what he was doing there*, she reminded herself.

She glanced surreptitiously at him. He was staring ahead. Silent. Dark. Brooding.

Something ricocheted off the hood of the jeep. She recognized it as a bullet just as a second one sliced through the air between them and exploded into the back seat.

Snipers!

Before she had a chance to react, Matt reached over and forced her head down. He slammed his foot hard on the gas and wrenched the steering wheel to the left. The jeep jumped off the road; it struggled valiantly but couldn't make it through the brush and rocky terrain.

He leapt out, one hand grabbing his backpack from the backseat, the other pulling her across the jeep and away from the road. Together, they headed up into the hills, toward what looked like a wooded area.

Another bullet whizzed past, landing inches from her ankle.

They ran swiftly. Matt held tightly to Julie's arm, urging her up the steep terrain. She felt the sting of branches slapping her face and the taste of copper as her own blood trickled into her mouth. Matt, however, was taking the brunt of the trees' resistance.

Finally, they slowed and stopped. Her chest was burning and she was panting heavily. Although she knew she was in great physical condition, it was obvious that regular workouts in a gym could not compare with the physical exertion that soldiers in the field experienced almost every day.

Her wrist was throbbing from his grasp and she rubbed it absently while she used her sleeve to wipe her face.

Matt was surveying their surroundings. The

forest had become less dense, but they were still well hidden from the road. She listened carefully but couldn't hear any sounds.

"Do you think they'll follow us?" she asked.

"I don't know. They have the jeep. That might be enough for them."

The jeep!

"You have your field radio, don't you? Call in our position. Master Sergeant Murray will have us out of here in no time."

Matt was already kneeling on the ground, examining the bullet hole that had pierced his pack. As he opened it and withdrew the large metallic box, he swore softly. The radio was useless. It had caught the bullet.

Great. That meant they'd have to walk back to base. It would be a long, arduous journey; they obviously couldn't take the road.

"All right," she checked her GPS and headed off, "the city is this way."

"Whoa! Major," Matt said, grabbing her arm. "We need to find a place to hole-up for the night and head out tomorrow morning."

"We can't do that. We have to get back. They'll be looking for us."

"And maybe they'll find us. But if we try to make it to the city tonight, for sure the bandits will find us first. We could stumble onto a road or a village at any point. These hills aren't as remote as they appear." He paused, then added, "With all due respect, Major. May I suggest that for tonight only we forego rank? I have no doubt that you're a first-rate commander, but I'll also lay odds that you haven't had much field experience. This is what I'm trained for, so how about I take the lead."

She knew he was right, yet she couldn't give up control of the situation. If she did, what would she have left?

"Negative, Lieutenant. I'll entertain suggestions, but the decisions are mine."

"Yes, ma'am," he snapped to attention. "This area is likely to have a number of caves and other natural shelters. I suggest we take a quick re-con to see if we can find something suitable for the night."

Julie looked up at the sky. It wouldn't be long before the light began fading. They needed to find something before darkness fell. "Fine, Lieutenant. Lead on."

****

Matt headed toward an outcropping of rocks further up the hill. He made sure his pace was slow enough for Julie to easily keep up on the rocky slope.

Great, just great. It was bad enough he could barely keep his thoughts off of her when she wasn't around, but now she was here with him, and he was having trouble focusing on keeping them both out of danger.

She had followed him? Why?

"Who do you think they are?" Her voice cut into his thoughts. "My reports haven't shown any rebels active in this area."

"They're probably not rebels. They're probably just criminals looking for an easy score."

"You think a jeep being driven by two military officers is an easy score?"

Matt kept his gaze forward, trying to formulate a palatable answer. After a few moments, he gave up. There was no way to sugar-coat their situation. "I think *they* would think that a jeep being driven by an Indian and a lady soldier would be an easy score."

He could tell Julie had stopped. He took a deep breath and turned to look at her. Her face was red with indignation. He didn't want to debate the pros and cons of women in the military. He'd been fighting his own battle against prejudice since signing up, and from the look of things, she had fared pretty well.

"I didn't say *I* agreed. I'm just giving you the facts, Major. This is a macho society. You can't bring our American values to the situation and expect them to work here."

"I know that! I'm just tired of always defending my gender."

"No one's asking you to defend anything, Major. I'm just saying that in the Beljouan mindset, we're easy pickings."

"What you're really saying is that this is my fault."

"I didn't say that," he said defensively.

"But you do think you would have been better off on your own—even walking."

He was on thin ice. He *knew* he would have been fine by himself, but did he dare tell her that? Whatever her reasons for following him, her arrival in full military regalia had jeopardized both of their lives. To tell her that, however, would only shake her confidence. He was angry with her, but not enough to hurt her. He'd done enough of that already.

Julie was expecting an answer. He couldn't tell her the truth, and he couldn't lie to her, either. "I look like one of the indigenous peoples here. If I'm not in uniform and I keep my mouth shut, no one can really tell the difference. The Indians are at the bottom of the social ladder in Beljou. So to most people here, I'm just another stupid Indian—not worth the trouble."

"Sounds like I hit a nerve."

He cursed inwardly. She had picked up on the bitterness he had tried to keep out of his tone. He had better put an end to the conversation. "No, ma'am," he said and began walking.

"Really?" She didn't move and he was forced to stop. "It sounds like this is more than just a commentary on Beljouan society. Do you think you, personally, are discriminated against because you're Native American?"

"I've nothing else to say on the matter." He tried to get them moving again, but she stubbornly remained rooted to her spot. He looked at her in exasperation. "We really should get going."

"I wonder why a man who is so concerned with being accepted as part of his community would rather have everyone believe he's a Casanova who seduces women for information rather than telling them the truth—that he's a good guy whose alter ego is Tim the Toolman."

"Tim the Toolman?"

"Yeah, you know, Tim the Toolman Taylor?" When he didn't reply, she continued, "Didn't you ever watch TV? *Home Improvement*?"

"I guess I missed that one." Matt didn't like the way the conversation was going, and yet he couldn't think of how to take it in another direction. At least she had started walking.

"You didn't have a TV growing up?"

"You mean on the reservation?" He didn't know what made him say that, but he could taste the bitterness of his words. The truth was he had never watched much TV because he could never identify with the characters. It was another thing that had alienated him from his classmates. He was feeling that same alienation now.

Julie gasped. "That's not what I meant. It's just that it was a very popular show. I was only trying to make conversation. What's biting your ass, Lieutenant?"

"Sorry, Major," Matt said. And he was. "I don't watch much TV. I've never found much on that's worth watching."

"Well, that's a whole other issue." She paused, and then continued, her voice softer. "Was it difficult? Growing up on a reservation, I mean."

Matt closed his eyes and swore softly. Well, he'd asked for it, hadn't he? "I didn't grow up on a reservation. My mother left it just after I was born. I grew up in Green Bay."

"Really? Green Bay, Wisconsin?"

"Yeah, I'm a real cheese-head."

"Why did your mother leave?"

"I don't know. Can we drop it?"

"Why? You know all about me. Can you blame me for being curious about you?"

"Are we back to that again?"

"Have we ever left it? Why is it so hard for you to talk about yourself? About what happened the night before we left?"

"Hold on, Major. Let me remind you that it was *I* who came to your office to talk about that night, when we first arrived here. You were all over my ass about it."

"True. But you never gave me a satisfactory answer. Why all the secrecy? Why didn't you tell me who you were?"

"You want to know the truth?"

"Yes!"

They stood facing each other, eyes intense, expectant. It wasn't the whine of the bullet that broke the tension, but the tiny shards of wood erupting from the tree beside them.

"Shit!" Matt pushed Julie in front of him, urging her up the hill. He'd use his body to block any gunfire.

Dammit, she'd done it again. She'd distracted him from his goal of keeping her safe. He needed to focus. He couldn't let it happen again.

****

They were moving quickly over very rough terrain. She was keeping pace quite nicely, Julie thought with a measure of pride.

Suddenly, she felt a sharp pain as she went over

on her ankle and then fell forward, grabbing at air.

Matt lunged forward, but was too late to stop her fall. He reached down to help her up.

She gasped from pain and everything went black for a moment. He held her as she slowly sank back to the ground. Then he knelt and began gently prodding her ankle. So close to him, she could see he was wounded, too. His shirt had soaked up quite a lot of blood at his shoulder. She reached out to touch it. He flinched.

"You've been shot," she said.

"I don't think it was the gunfire," he smiled sheepishly. "I think it's wood shards. Not quite as glamorous. Anyway, it's only a graze. I'll look at it when we've found some shelter. But your ankle... I don't think it's broken, but you've got a nasty sprain."

"Just give me a second and I'll be okay," she said. If he could bear his injuries, so could she. She tried to rise, but the searing pain made her drop, again, to the ground.

"Let me take a look at that."

"But the bandits. They could be right behind us. We've got to keep moving."

"Yeah. Okay." He adjusted his pack and then swung her up over his shoulder.

"What are you doing?" She was indignant.

"We don't have a lot of time to argue, Major. We've got to find a place to hole up for tonight. You can't walk, so you'll just have to enjoy the ride."

Julie knew she was beaten. As he continued up the hill it was too uncomfortable to leave her arms dangling towards the ground so she resigned herself to placing them on his hips, and smiled with satisfaction as she felt him stiffen at her touch.

After a while, he slowed, and then stopped. Julie arched her back, trying to raise her head to see what was going on.

"What?" she whispered.

"A shelter and a cooking fire. There are only a few of them. I'm just going to put you down here, next to this rock, and see if I can get us some food."

"You're thinking of food? Now?"

He chuckled. "Food, and information."

"How do you know they aren't with the bandits?" Julie peered around the rock. Down a mild slope she could see smoke dancing up from a small fire. There were two figures moving around, oblivious to their presence.

Matt pulled his Beretta out of his waistband and checked it over. Satisfied, he replaced it and then responded. "I don't know for certain, but it's a risk we'll have to take. You can provide backup."

Julie looked at her swollen ankle. "A lot of good I'll be."

"You have your gun?"

"Of course."

"I'll bet you're a crack shot."

"Five-seventy-two out of a perfect six."

"Thought so."

She threw him a look of thanks. She wasn't totally helpless; she could contribute to the mission. Although, really, if she thought about it, how much help could she be if Matt ran into trouble down there?

She needn't have worried. She watched as he was greeted warmly by the two figures. They showed no hesitation in inviting him to join their fire and handed him a cup and plate. She couldn't hear what they were saying but could detect no hostility in their voices.

As time went on, she found herself becoming more and more annoyed. Her ankle was throbbing and, as the smell of food wafted up from the fire, her stomach's rumbling was becoming pronounced. Maybe Matt was right about needing food, after all.

Finally, she saw him rise, accept a small bundle, and head back up the hill towards her. She pushed herself closer to the rock in case the strangers' gazes followed him. It was ridiculous, she knew. In the waning light she'd just appear as another shadow.

Matt, however, didn't seem to be taking any chances, either, and walked past without acknowledging her. He rounded the rock and stopped just out of sight.

"Wait a minute," he whispered. "Let them return to their fire."

After a few minutes, he slipped back around the rock and lifted her into his arms. He didn't flip her over his shoulder as he had done before but carried her as a husband does a new bride. He had his backpack slipped over one shoulder and the bundle of food tied around the other.

Julie watched his face as he carried her along a rocky slope. He was grim.

"Well?" she asked.

"They barely had enough to feed themselves, but insisted I take something for my journey."

Matt's jaw was clenched, and Julie could see the veins in his neck, tight and pulsing.

"When we're out of this, we can come back and do something for them."

He didn't respond. She realized this must be the type of situation he encountered all the time. He and the others in his unit actually met and got to know the people she just read about in reports.

"They did say that something's up," he said. "They've come up from the south—to escape the revolutionaries, they say. But I think they're here for something else."

"Do you think the attack by the bandits could be something more, too?"

"I don't know, yet."

They continued on in silence until Julie's

stomach gave a great roar of discontent.

Matt's eyes opened in surprised and he looked down at her.

"Excuse me," she said sheepishly.

"My apologies, Major. It's taking a bit longer to find some place suitable, but I think I see something just across that ravine."

It turned out to be a small shelter, one of the many in the hills around the capital that had been built and abandoned by rural villagers looking for a better life in the city.

When they were several yards away, Matt set Julie down on the ground to investigate. The sun had totally set, and her eyes had adjusted to the darkness. Through the dimness, she watched him approach the shelter slowly, his gun drawn. He opened the door and disappeared inside. Julie held her breath and then sighed with relief as he emerged a few moments later.

He quickly strode back, hoisted her up again and carried her into the shelter. Inside was darker than outside; in the increased darkness, all Julie could make out was that it was a single room.

Matt carefully placed her on the floor and handed her the bundle of food. She fumbled blindly with the knot, finally opening it to reveal a stale bun and a morsel of roasted meat from an unknown animal. Julie didn't care. She was starving.

Matt removed his backpack and stretched broadly. He knelt beside Julie, withdrew a small flashlight from the pack and began to carefully remove her boot and sock.

Julie held her breath trying to block the pain. The ankle was turning purple and had almost doubled in size. "Sorry, no ice," Matt said. "I'll elevate it and see what I can find to bind it up." He removed a piece of clothing from the backpack—his military jacket—and balled it up as a support for her foot.

"Let me look at your shoulder," she said, reluctant to be the only patient.

He glanced nonchalantly at his shoulder, shrugged and then removed his shirt. Upon closer inspection, Julie saw that despite the amount of blood, it really was just a small graze.

"I don't suppose you have any antiseptic in your bag of tricks," she said.

"As a matter of fact, I do." He pulled a small bottle of rum out of the backpack. "Good for all that ails you," he said taking a sip. Then he poured some of the rum onto the sleeve of his shirt, but instead of applying it to his shoulder he leaned toward Julie and began gently to clean the cuts on her face.

She took the bottle from him and poured more of the rum onto the other sleeve of his shirt and began dabbing his shoulder. She had to brace herself by putting her other hand on his chest. His heart was racing and she could feel his warm, rapid breath on her cheek. She was having difficulty breathing, too. He circled his good arm around her back to hold her steady. She stiffened, and then relaxed to focus on cleaning his wound.

She couldn't stop thinking about his nearness and the stirring in her body. Memories came flooding back to her: Matt holding her tightly, each of their bodies pressing closer and closer as if they could become one; the taste of his mouth on hers; the feel of his tongue as it glided along her neck to the opening of her shirt; his hands...

Stop! She jerked back and Matt winced.

"Sorry," she said and tried to cover her confusion by resuming her ministrations of his shoulder. But her quick motions just seemed to cause more pain and he took the shirt from her.

"That's fine, thanks," he said, pulling his shirt over his head. "We'll be fine here tonight," he said, the concern on his face belying the calm of his voice.

"I really did botch things up, didn't I?" In thinking about their situation, she was beginning to realize just how big a liability she was. She had wanted this overseas assignment so much—maybe too much. Perhaps the senior command knew she couldn't hack it and that was why they had waited so long to give it to her. There was a big difference between running a mission from The Room in Fort Bragg, and actually being here on the ground, seeing the lives of the people you were supposedly helping.

"It's fine. We'll be fine," he said.

Well, what else would he say? Then: *Get a grip, Jules. You are here because you deserve to be here. Don't you dare wallow in self-pity.*

She struggled for something to say that would help her feel like less of a screw-up. She should apologize for her earlier comments about his heritage. "Look," she began hesitantly, "I'm sorry about before. I didn't mean to bug you about... you know... where you came from."

Julie could see Matt's eyebrows rise quizzically. Damn! She was making a mess of this, too.

"Don't worry about it. I probably over-reacted."

"No, it was really insensitive of me. I'm..."

Her words were cut off as Matt's lips claimed hers. Julie felt all breath rush out of her lungs as a jolt of electricity sizzled through her body.

Matt's lips were gentle at first; softly brushing her own, barely a whisper against her mouth. She knew she should resist, but didn't want to. Then the pressure increased and she felt his tongue demand entry. She really should stop him. This wasn't appropriate.

She yielded, savoring the sensation of his tongue as it explored every crevice of her mouth. She reached up to grasp his head. Her fingers tangled themselves in the dark, silky hair, and she pulled him closer, deepening their kiss.

Matt moaned, deep and low, and she could hear him calling her name, deep inside her. His arms encircled her.

She arched towards him, aching to feel every inch of his body next to hers. Her fingers moved from his head, her thumbs stroking the sharp edge delineating his cheekbone. His skin was firm and smooth.

Matt placed a hand behind her head and his body pushed her backwards, laying her down onto the warm ground. Hovering over her, he cupped her face with his one hand and began to slowly, sensually glide his fingers down her face, along her neck, to the top of her shirt. His lips followed, licking and nibbling until she couldn't think anymore. The heat and wetness between her legs made her body cry out for fulfillment.

Instinctively, she tried to pull him down to her—she needed to feel his hard body on hers. As she reached towards him, her world exploded in a blinding flash of throbbing red agony, and she cried out.

Matt immediately backed away and jumped to his feet.

She rolled back, one hand raking her short hair, angrily. *What do you think you're doing, Jules?* "I'm sorry," she recovered quickly, although her breath was still ragged. Hopefully, he'd think it was from the pain of her ankle. "That was entirely inappropriate. I should know better."

Matt looked down at her, his expression unreadable. "That's all right." His voice was rough. "It's just the adrenalin looking for some release. It happens all the time after combat."

"Really? You mean soldiers run around kissing each other after a battle? That's quite an image." Julie rued her habit of resorting to humor—very bad humor—when she was stressed. The trait aggravated her father. That was its only benefit.

Matt, however, seemed to take it in stride.

"Well, I guess it all depends on how attracted you are to the fellas in your unit," he said, his eyes dancing mischievously. "Unfortunately, Brownwell and Wilkes aren't really my type, so I've had to settle for plain old macho back-slapping and high-fiving."

"Poor you." Julie struggled to sit up. She appreciated his effort to downplay what had happened. Her head knew they were right to stop, but regret gnawed at her restless body.

"You wait here. I'll just do a quick re-con to make sure everything's copasetic." Matt removed his night goggles from the backpack and checked his sidearm.

Julie nodded. She needed a bit of time away from him to sort out her thoughts. She unsheathed her Browning and laid it across her lap. "Just in case I meet one of the local *lwas*," she said in reply to his inquiring look.

Her sudden lightheadedness was not the result of his soft chuckle of amused admiration, she told herself. It was simply her body's response to the throbbing of her ankle.

"There's water in the canteen," he said.

The door of the hut closed. She was alone.

With the sun down, the air had turned cool. It was unpleasant and damp. She shivered.

This has not been a banner day, Jules.

What was it about Matthew Wolf that made her throw all good sense and reason to the wind? She had always been so careful in her choices—in her actions. She needed to stay away from him.

Now that she had solved the mystery about his intelligence-gathering tactics, she could let him go back to Cap-Verte without another thought. Or could she?

In some ways she had hoped she would find him in a compromising situation. If she could prove to herself that he was dishonorable—that he had been using her—then she could dismiss him and move on. Yet, she couldn't deny the relief she felt when she'd learned the truth. It didn't explain everything. It didn't explain why he had lied to her or what he wanted from her.

Part of her wanted to hate him. To find a reason to hate him. She hadn't found that today. Instead, she gleaned a bit more information about the mysterious Lieutenant Wolf. He genuinely cared about the people of Beljou—it was more than just trying to make inroads with them to do his job. Port-au-Paix wasn't his district. He didn't have to spend his time off helping the villagers here, playing with their children. There was no doubt that his visit today would go a long way toward helping Captain Wilkes, but Julie doubted that had even entered Matt's mind.

She supposed she really shouldn't be surprised by his actions. At the briefing earlier, he had spoken passionately about the people of the island, the hardships they had to bear and their enduring spirit. This was the man she remembered from their night together in Fayetteville.

She sensed something else in him, too, and it was disquieting. There seemed to be a bitterness about his past, his Native American heritage, that she hadn't expected. She was surprised by his reaction to her comments about discrimination, and then to her questions about growing up on a reservation...

Damn, Jules. You'd think in your position you would be a bit more sensitive.

She started as she heard the distinctive click of a gun being cocked just behind her ear.

"Do not make a sound, Madame."

And everything went black.

CHAPTER 5

Matt slowly opened the door of the hut so that he wouldn't startle Julie.

"Major?" he whispered.

Silence.

"Major!" A little louder.

His heartbeat quickened and he unsheathed his Beretta. He pushed the door a little wider, listening intently for any sound, even the soft breath of slumber, as unlikely as that was. Nothing except the deafening roar of the cicadas outside. His vision had adjusted to the night sky, but the inside of the hut was much darker. He stepped back, allowing the door to swing softly shut.

OH-tuh!

He slipped on the night visor. He didn't want to risk anything brighter than that. The beam of a flashlight would be visible from a great distance. He flipped the switch and the visor illuminated a gentle green glow. He removed the safety from his gun and eased his way back into the hut.

As he feared, the hut was empty. Nevertheless, he moved slowly, catlike, across the room, listening carefully for any sound that didn't belong, looking for some clue as to what had happened to Julie.

He bent down to more closely examine the place where he'd left her. His heart almost stopped as he spotted a few droplets of blood. But no, that was his blood. He instinctively touched his shoulder and winced at the pain.

The floor looked like it had been swept recently; the only visible footprints were his. If there had been a struggle, it had been well covered up. At least inside.

Matt walked the perimeter of the shelter. The ground had been trampled. It looked like whoever had been here had circled the building a few times. He could identify two distinct sets of footprints—neither of which bore the mark of army treads.

He forced down the unfamiliar burn of bile rising in his throat, and willed his heartbeat to slow. He couldn't think straight if he was panicking. And he couldn't help Julie if he wasn't thinking straight.

You're trained for this. This is just another mission. But he knew that wasn't true. He'd been involved in many rescues of his fellow soldiers, both women and men. Unfortunately, Julie wasn't just *any* soldier. She was a C.O. And she was the daughter of the Army Chief of Staff. And she was... well, he couldn't go there. Not if he was going to be of any use to her.

Okay, Boyo, let's put that million-dollar training to use.

How long had he left her? Twenty minutes? That gave them a bit of a head start. But where had they gone? The footprints didn't seem to lead in any particular direction.

The moon, just past full, slipped out from behind a cloud. Matt removed the visor and scanned the surrounding hillside. The rocky terrain obscured the bandits' tracks.

Think, Boyo. Think!

A scurrying sound off to his right made him drop to his knees, roll up close to the hut and aim his gun. He paused, waiting. He heard it again, but it was too small to be human. Still, he didn't move, willing the cloud to reclaim the moon's bright rays. He felt exposed.

Then he saw it. A large, mangy brown dog was tentatively approaching, its body slung low to the ground. Matt held his breath. Wild dogs usually ran in packs.

The dog moved cautiously, its body rigid and eyes intent. Matt's gun followed the animal's approach. Logic told him he should just shoot. He waited.

The dog stopped a few paces from him, sat, and did nothing. Slowly he let out his breath. He rose, keeping the gun trained on the animal. It remained still. Matt took a step towards it. The dog cocked its head to one side and let out a soft whine. As he got closer, he recognized the animal. It belonged to James, the boy from the village he had left a few hours earlier.

He lowered the gun and held out his hand. The dog came to him, sniffed briefly and then turned its head for Matt to scratch.

"Well, my brother," he said, a smile coming involuntarily to his lips, "what brings you here? Do you have a story to tell me?"

If this was James' dog, that meant he must still be relatively near Mama Sophie's village. And if that was the case, what were the odds that Mama Sophie knew something about who had taken Julie?

"Well, boy," he said, giving the dog one last deep scratch behind the ears, "time for you to get home. And time for me to see how much Mama Sophie really likes me. Come on, boy. Home."

Although Matt spoke in English, the dog seemed to understand. It rose and headed off at a slow trot, back in the direction from which it came. It kept a steady pace, pausing occasionally to make sure Matt was following.

The dog didn't follow any fixed path and Matt had difficulty keeping his footing. Once he lost it completely and slid several yards down the hill amid a shower of stones and vegetation. The dog waited patiently while he scrambled back up, and then set off again.

After about forty-five minutes they crested the top of a small hill. Matt recognized the collection of houses below and the road he had used earlier in the day. There was no movement.

He looked at his watch. Ten-thirty. He couldn't very well go down into the village at this time of night, he decided, fighting back a wave of frustration. While he doubted Julie was there, he would keep awake to watch for any signs of activity. In the morning—probably best after the men had left for the city—he'd go down and see what the women knew.

Matt sat with his back against a rock face where he could keep an eye on the village and be aware of anyone approaching from the hill behind him. The rock had already absorbed the cool night air and he shifted uncomfortably. His jacket, along with the rest of his gear, had disappeared with Julie.

The dog lay down beside him, resting its head on his lap, and Matt absently petted him.

He had an affinity for dogs, although he had never owned one as a pet. His mother said it was a crime to keep them confined in the city; they belonged in a place where they could have more freedom to run and hunt. He had surreptitiously adopted a number of the neighborhood dogs, sneaking into backyards to play with them and give them treats without their owners—or his mother—being aware of it.

Matt knew that his own name, Wolf, was not the name he was born with. His mother had claimed it for them, one of the few things she took with her when she left the reservation. They were members of the Oneida Nation's Wolf clan.

His grandparents had taught him what little he knew about native traditions. He could hear his grandfather, rocking back and forth, hypnotically, in the kitchen of his home on the reservation, while his grandmother fussed in the background.

"Be proud of your birthright, Matthew," he would say. "You are part of a great nation, a great clan. The Wolf clan. We are the keepers of fire and the holders of knowledge. It is the Wolf that gives us direction on the pathway of life. It is the Wolf that leads us to live in the way the Creator wished for us. It is the Wolf that gives us respect for the importance of family, teaches us to use our ears and be watchful, just as a family does for its members. In nature, the Wolf seeks out and explores new situations to find new knowledge and returns with it to the pack. The Wolf has great curiosity, and while he might explore on his own, he will return to the pack, preferring the company of others."

Except for the part about preferring the company of others, Matt believed his grandfather was right; he was a wolf. He wondered what the old man would think of his chosen profession.

Sometimes his grandmother would take him aside and add, "The Wolf, Matthew, is a great responsibility. For the Wolf is a creature of passion, of sympathy and of understanding. These are qualities possessed by our clan. It is to the Wolf clan that others turn in times of need. You must know this and learn to use it wisely."

Of course, he didn't really understand any of it at the time. He had been just a kid when they died. But as he grew older, their words would often come back to him. He wished he could have asked his mother about it, but that subject and anything to do with her past was closed.

As the sun began its ascent, Matt's senses heightened. His ears strained for any sound coming from the village, his eyes searched for movement among the houses. He could see smoke from cooking fires and his stomach rumbled as he caught the scent of breakfast. He still had candy in his pocket, although he thought it best to save it for currency with the villagers.

He stretched his neck, shoulders and arms, and readjusted his position, but didn't rise. The dog, disturbed by his movement, or perhaps tempted by the smells from the village, got up, stretched languidly and sauntered down the hill.

"Sure, choose a few morsels of meat over me," Matt said, his voice gravelly from lack of sleep. "Just don't give me away when I show up there."

As the minutes slowly ticked by, he saw women emerge from their homes to get water and begin their numerous morning activities. Children, too, came to help. Then, last of all, the men emerged, stretching and scratching.

A big, colorful bus rambled along the road to the village, coughing black smoke. It stopped, collected the men, and then headed back down the hill toward Port-au-Paix. He watched until it disappeared.

Now.

He rose, slid the Beretta into the waistband of his pants and covered it with his shirt. The night visor? He had nowhere to hide it. Well, he'd just have to leave it here and retrieve it later.

Matt's reception at the village was as hospitable as his departure had been. If they were surprised to see him return so soon, they gave no indication of it. James led a gang of children who rushed toward him, all with their hands extended in anticipation of candy. The women smiled shyly and waved as he passed.

He knocked softly on Mama Sophie's door. He heard the scraping of a chair along the floor and what he thought were hushed voices inside. He had to stop himself from rushing the hut. He couldn't afford to alienate Mama Sophie. Finally, the door opened.

"Ah, Lieutenant Matthew Wolf," she said,

drawing out every syllable of his name. "This is a surprise. I hadn't expected to see you again so soon."

She made no attempt to move. Was she deliberately trying to delay, giving time for someone inside to escape? But no, there was no rear exit to the building. Matt had checked for that when he was here before. He tried to peer discreetly around her, but the hut was too dimly lit and the day too bright for his eyes to see anything.

"Mama Sophie," he gave her a brilliant smile, "I have a matter I must urgently discuss with you. May I come in?"

The woman stepped back, allowing him to enter. He paused on the threshold to give his eyes time to adjust and then quickly scanned the room. A candle, the only light, burned in a corner. He couldn't see anything—or anyone—that hadn't been there the day before.

She was already heading toward the table and picking up the bottle of rum.

"Oh, no, Mama," Matt said swiftly, shaking his head. The last thing he needed on an empty stomach was alcohol. "Perhaps some fruit?" he suggested, eying a basket in the corner.

She snorted in derision, motioned for him to help himself, and proceeded to pour herself a generous glass of rum. She floated over to her chair and slowly descended into a seated position.

Matt didn't want to sit—he was too agitated—but he knew standing would be construed as rude, so he took his former chair facing the woman. She was dressed in the same clothes as the day before. Come to think of it, so was he. It was as if no time had passed. But of course it had. A whole world of time had passed. Julie had been taken, and he needed desperately to find out anything he could. Still, Mama Sophie was a mambo and protocol dictated that he wait until she spoke first.

Mama Sophie seemed intent on her drink. She inhaled deeply and then downed it in a single gulp. Matt was afraid she was going to get up and pour herself another glass, but she didn't. She placed the glass on the table beside her, folded her hands across her large belly and pursed her lips. Finally, she spoke.

"So, Lieutenant Matthew Wolf, you have a problem and you think Mama Sophie can help solve it for you." It was more of a statement than a question.

"Yes, Mama. I am certain that you, with your wisdom, will be able to help me."

She smiled. "You flatter me, but go ahead."

"When I left here yesterday, I was met by a woman. A military woman, and we left together in a jeep."

"Ah yes, I heard about this woman from my girls. They were very jealous, Lieutenant Matthew Wolf. They thought she was your wife. Of course, I told them no. A man like Lieutenant Matthew Wolf would not have a wife."

Her words stung. Matt had never thought about marriage, yet hearing Mama Sophie dismiss the idea so bluntly was disturbing. He wanted to ask her why, but forced himself to stay on topic. She was cunning. Matt needed to keep his wits about him. He couldn't allow her to distract him.

"No, she's not my wife. She's my commanding officer." He ignored another of Sophie's derisive snorts. On Beljou it was the men who held the outward signs of power while women controlled subtly from behind. A woman openly in command of a man—a real man—was unthinkable to the people of Beljou.

"Our country is not like yours," he continued. "Where I come from, women and men share equally in power."

Sophie rolled her eyes in disbelief. Truth was, Matt wasn't sure he really believed it, either, but this definitely wasn't the time to discuss equality issues. He'd just have to ignore Sophie's reaction and hope it didn't diminish him in her eyes.

"On the road to Port-au-Paix our jeep was shot at by bandits, and she was taken hostage."

"*Mondu*! How terrible!" Sophie's hands flew to her face and her eyes grew wide with mock horror. She was acting. He knew it; and what was worse, she knew he knew it and she didn't care.

"Have there been bandits in this area who might harbor a grudge towards the army? Any that would be bold enough to risk retaliation from America?"

"It is not a matter of grudges or of boldness, Lieutenant Matthew Wolf. You should know that. It is a matter of honor and survival. It is a matter of life and death." She paused and looked longingly at the empty glass beside her. "I know of no such group. I cannot help you."

Matt bit down on the bile of despair that rose from his stomach and threatened to overwhelm him. If Mama Sophie wouldn't help him, he was at a dead end here. He rose to go.

"Mama Sophie, I thank you for your hospitality and the service you have done for us already. If, for some reason, some piece of information comes to you that may help us find Major Collins, please send word to the American compound."

Sophie remained seated, her head turned from Matt as he left. The village seemed deserted. No children ran to greet him. No women waved. Only one long, lanky dog came to say goodbye.

As he climbed the hill to retrieve his night visor he tried to figure out his next move. He had nothing. His only option was to return to the compound and pass on what little he knew to the command there. They'd send him back south to complete his mission while they... What? What would they do?

Matt and Julie had been missing overnight. While he wasn't surprised no one came after him, he was very surprised no alarm seemed to have been raised about Julie's disappearance. Surely they knew where she went? Hadn't she said Jimmy had given her the directions? Why had no one from the compound come to the village to search for her?

He bent down to pick up the night visor and turned back toward the road that led to Port-au-Paix.

Alone, dressed as he was, he wasn't afraid of being attacked, but he definitely had the feeling he was being watched. He turned suddenly and caught a brief flight of movement. He felt for his gun.

"Okay. I know you're there. Come on out."

He half expected to see that crazy dog again, but instead, slowly, from behind an outcrop of rocks emerged one of the women from the village, and James.

"Sorry, no more candy," he called, annoyed.

"Please, *monsieur*," the woman said, hurrying towards him. She looked nervous. James ran happily beside her, a big grin splitting his face.

Matt was used to this. Many of the poorer village women thought that he could somehow save them from whatever fate they were facing. The best he could do was to take her to the compound and see if they could find a job for her. *OH-tuh!* They'd slow him down. Still, he couldn't turn his back on her.

"How can I help you, madame?"

"It's my son. He knows something that can help you."

Matt's heart skipped a beat, but he remained nonchalant. He didn't want to spook them. He waited.

"Last night, I went outside to pee and I heard *Grandpère*. He was yelling at my uncles, calling them stupid and idiots." James looked anxiously at his mother. Obviously these were words he wasn't supposed to say. When he saw she wasn't going to chastise him, he continued, relishing the opportunity to say the forbidden words. "He said, 'You are all stupid fools. I gave you two of them and you only took one. And the woman, no less. You did not wait for the man to return and take him, too.' And then he said, 'I am surrounded by idiots.'"

Matt stood stone still. So it wasn't a random act. He and Julie had been targeted. But why? How?

"Thank you, James," he reached into his pocket and handed over his remaining supply of candy. James gave a piece to his mother.

Matt turned to the woman. Although she was probably only in her twenties, she looked much older. There was a gray pallor to her skin and silver threads in her dark hair. Her dark brown eyes looked tired and her shoulders stooped from too much labor.

"I thank you for this information, but why tell me? What is it you want from me in return?"

The woman lowered her head. "My husband is dead. He died when the violence began two years ago. Mama Sophie is my husband's mother. James is her only grandchild. Her own daughter cannot bear children. While he is dear to her heart, I am not." She looked at her son and smiled. Somehow he had managed to get candy on his forehead. She licked her thumb and scrubbed at the sugary trail while James grimaced with embarrassment. "Mama Sophie is growing old and losing her control, not only on the women but on Papa, her own husband. If something were to happen to her, her daughter would become the Mama. She would take my son from me."

"Do you know where they have taken Major Collins?"

She nodded, but remained silent. The negotiation was on.

"I believe I can help you and your son." Matt reached into his pocket and withdrew a card. On the back he wrote a message. "If you tell me where I may find Major Collins, I will give you this card. You will take this card to the compound in Port-au-Paix and give it to Master Sergeant Murray. He will help you find employment, and a safe place for you and your son."

"Not in the kitchens!"

Matt's eyebrows rose, surprised by the vehemence of her words. Come to think of it, most of the people working in the kitchen were men. Maybe there was a cultural taboo he wasn't aware of.

"You won't have to work in the kitchens if you don't want to. There are a lot of jobs at the compound."

He held up the card. She hesitated, but only for a moment. "Through the southern mountains—Cap-Verte. Papa has many relatives there. Many people who will help him."

Matt handed her the card. "Thank you, madame."

She nodded and gathered her son to her. "You are not returning to your compound?"

"No, I'm going directly to Cap-Verte."

****

Everything was black, yet her eyes were open. Julie was sure they were open. She blinked several times, but the darkness remained.

Her head was pounding and there was a bitter taste of something acidic in her mouth. She licked her lips and winced as the moisture of her tongue met the parched skin.

She could tell from the jostling that she was in a vehicle, every bounce set off a wave of nausea as her ankle struck something hard.

What's going on? Where am I going?

As the words formed in her mind, she realized she didn't really care. She was tired... so desperately tired...

****

She awoke with a start. It was daytime. Thin rays of light were slipping through slats in the wall and slicing across the floor. Julie remained immobile, trying to figure out what had happened.

Without raising her head—she wasn't sure she could anyway—she scanned the room. It was small, no more than ten feet across. There was a door at one end, towards her feet. No windows.

She was lying on something. A cot? It was hard, and something was digging into her hip. She tried to shift position and heard a jangle of clanging metal.

What the...?

She sat up quickly. Everything went black for an instant as blinding pain shot simultaneously through her head and ankle. Slowly, she lowered herself again. Reaching down to her hip, she fingered the heavy metal links of a chain and followed it down, down to a thick band that was wrapped around her uninjured ankle.

Her heart was pounding and she had to fight down the sickening wave of panic.

Calm yourself, Jules. Use your training.

She closed her eyes and took several deep breaths. There was a damp, musty smell in the air that was different from what she had become accustomed to in Port-au-Paix. Here, there was no smell of exhaust fumes from the thousands of poorly maintained vehicles that clogged the city's streets. She couldn't smell the sea, either.

Okay, so we're inland somewhere—away from the capital.

She listened. There were birds. And, very faintly, voices. She held her breath and tried to hear what they were saying. They were male voices. Two? No, three distinct voices. But they were too far away to make out the words. She heard an engine turn over and a vehicle drive away. Then everything was quiet. Was she alone?

She glanced at her watch to see how long she had been out. It was gone. She did a quick pat down of herself just to confirm what she already knew—she had been thoroughly searched. Her gun and the knife she kept strapped to her calf had been removed. Her pockets were empty. *Damn!* They took her drawing of the *vèvè*. She never had gotten around to showing it to Matt. And wasn't that how this whole thing had started? Finding Matt to show him the newest *vèvè* was what prompted her to follow him.

Really, Jules? Her conscience wasn't about to let her get away with that lame excuse. That's what the *vèvè* was—an excuse. *Now look where you are.* She needed to get out of here.

She grabbed the links of the chain and slowly began to pull them towards her. It was a long chain—long enough for her to get from one side of the room to the other. The chain suddenly tightened and she could pull it no more. Keeping hold, she slid to the floor and followed it under the bench to where it left the room through a hole at the base of the wall.

She wrapped the chain around her hands, braced her good foot against the wall and pulled with all her strength. The chain remained strong.

"Ahhhh!" she cried in frustration.

She heard running footsteps and a door opening. The steps drew closer and suddenly her door flew open to reveal a man with a red bandana covering his face and holding an automatic rifle—Julie recognized it as an M-16, the kind used by the American military.

"Get away from there!"

It was the same voice she had heard just before everything went black.

She didn't take her eyes off the man and slowly rose, keeping her hands in plain sight. He stepped towards her, motioning her to the bench with the rifle. She limped backwards, keeping as much weight off her sore ankle as possible, and sat down when she felt the bench touch the back of her calves.

"Who are you? Why am I here?" Her voice was firm and commanding; at the same time her mind was racing. Was this a military action or one of the more criminal elements operating in the country? She needed information.

She tried to commit every detail of the man to memory. He was shorter than her, she was pretty sure of that. His eyes—the only part of his face she could really see—were a pasty brown and held the look of a man desperately relishing the power he currently held over her. *Enjoy it now, buddy, because as soon as I get out of here, I'm coming after you!* His thick curly black hair was cut short. There was nothing really distinguishing about the man. But she would remember him.

"Don't speak to me, woman!"

He brought the muzzle of the rifle closer to her. She didn't flinch, her eyes never left his. It seemed to unnerve him—exactly what she was hoping for. Her hands were free. She could jump up, overpower him and grab the rifle. Would her ankle hold? Well, she couldn't—wouldn't—just sit here and do nothing.

She sat very still, preparing her body and mind. *Three... two... now!* She jumped up, surprising the man and lunged for the rifle. She swung the barrel towards his face and, as it made contact, his hands loosened their grip and she was able to wrestle it from him. She swung it at him again, hard, knocking him unconscious.

A gunshot echoed around the room and she whirled toward the door, aiming the rifle at the two figures entering. One sprang towards her, ducking low; he tackled her just as she got off a shot. With her ankle still throbbing, Julie's balance was precarious at best and, as the man made contact, she fell heavily. Her bullet fired uselessly into the ceiling and the rifle fell from her grip and slid out of reach. She grabbed the chain and quickly wrapped it around her assailant's neck.

"Please, madame, this is so unnecessary. You are quite outnumbered."

Julie had become so accustomed to hearing and understanding Beljouan Creole—thanks to Suzanne's lessons—that it took a moment for her to realize the man still standing in the doorway was speaking to her in English.

He was very tall, and was made all the more intimidating by the hideous mask he wore. It was a blue dragon's face with large red horns and a yellow snake captured in its enormous white teeth. She wouldn't allow him to frighten her. The pistol he had fired now hung casually by his side. He wasn't even aiming it at her.

"I think I'm holding my own," she said tightening her grip on the man struggling against the chain.

The man chuckled, a surprisingly pleasant sound given the circumstances. "You Americans! So arrogant."

"If you want to save your man's life, you better give me some answers." She further tightened the chain around the man's neck, adding emphasis to her words. The man squealed in protest.

"His life is of no consequence. A casualty of war." The man shrugged and waved his pistol nonchalantly.

"Really?" She felt a rising fear in her prisoner; he knew the man at the door was serious, then. "And just what war would that be?"

The masked man didn't reply.

"Where am I? What's going on? Do you know who I am?" she persisted. Answers. She desperately needed answers.

"Oh yes, Major Collins, I know who you are. As for where you are, that, I am afraid, I cannot reveal. And what else? Oh yes, what is going on? Well, think of yourself as my guest—at least for the time being."

"And you call me arrogant? I'm the one holding your man, here."

"Ah, yes." The masked man at the door took two quick steps into the room and kicked Julie's sore ankle. She winced at the pain, but didn't loosen her grip on the chains. He bent down and grabbed her ankle, twisting it painfully. This time, she couldn't help herself; it was all she could do not to black out.

The moment he felt the pressure slacken, the man on the floor jumped to his feet and disengaged himself from the chain. Then he raced to grab the rifle that had been dropped earlier and turned on Julie.

"*Arrête!*" The masked man shouted and then continued in a dialect Julie was unable to follow. It wasn't the Creole Suzanne had been teaching her. It must be indigenous to this region, she thought. The two men spoke angrily for a few moments and then the former hostage lowered the rifle, grabbed the unconscious man by the arm and dragged him from the room.

"As I said, think of yourself as my guest," the masked man said, switching back to English and waving his hand as if he were showing her the features of a high-class hotel suite. "I will have someone bring you something to eat and drink shortly. In the meantime, you should probably rest. You look a little pale."

Suddenly he threw his head back and gave a loud

throaty laugh. The snake between the dragon's teeth writhed sickeningly, as if alive. Then he turned and walked from the room. She heard a lock slide into place.

Julie raised her gaze to the ceiling and cursed her stupidity. *Come on, Jules. You're supposed to be an accomplished officer. Thank God the General can't see you now!*

She had to fight back the tears of frustration welling in her eyes. *Soldiers don't cry!* She'd get out of this—somehow.

It wasn't as if she was alone on Beljou. Surely someone would raise the alarm when she didn't return to the compound. Jimmy would be able to tell them where she went. They'd come after her. Beljou wasn't that big of an island. The American military wasn't about to let one of its commanders be kidnapped.

Buoyed with confidence that she would eventually be rescued—oh, how Julie hated that she had to be—she turned her thoughts to what had happened to Matt. Had he been ambushed when he returned to the hut? She didn't know why, but she was fairly certain he hadn't been.

Intuition was something she vehemently rejected; yet she had the strangest sense that he was okay and that he was coming to get her. Although she barely knew the man, she knew in her soul that he'd move heaven and earth to find her. She shivered with anticipation at the thought.

CHAPTER 6

Matt clung to lucidity. He'd barely slept for the last three days, only managing an hour here and there as he caught the occasional ride. In true Beljou fashion, the people he met had been generous with their limited provisions. He hadn't eaten like a king, but he had eaten.

He never traveled with any one person for very long. While he was certain he could maintain the impression he was a native Beljouan over the short-term, longer contact was riskier. In the south, the bandits would have a good network of spies. They'd be expecting him.

Despite the ineptitude of the actual kidnappers, Matt was certain the mastermind of the plot had a well-defined plan. A ransom note would arrive at the compound almost immediately. But they had taken Julie and not him. Would that alter their plans?

Matt mentally calculated, again, how long it would take for the military to mobilize its resources and attempt a rescue of Julie. It would take James' mother several days to trust Murray enough to expose her son to his interrogation. Then the army would have to devise a plan and take it through the appropriate channels. They'd have to secure agreement from the Beljou president—they were here at his invitation and couldn't risk an incident. The president, wanting to demonstrate his autonomy, would equivocate for a time. How long? Not long enough to irritate America. Twenty-four hours? So that gave him, maybe, five days to find her and get her to safety.

But then again, Julie wasn't an ordinary military officer. Her father was the Army Chief of Staff with a direct line to the Defense Secretary and the President. Matt could plan and estimate all he wanted, but all bets were off where she was concerned. And that was what really concerned him.

His initial decision not to tell Murray about Julie's whereabouts had been impulsive. She was Matt's responsibility and he should rescue her. But as he contemplated it more, he was confident he'd made the right call. Cap-Verte was a powder keg that could explode at the slightest provocation. If it did, many innocent people would lose their lives. They were so close to bringing safety back to the ordinary citizens, he was afraid if the army rolled in now, with guns a-blazing, all that had been accomplished to gain their trust would be lost, and the region would descend into lawlessness. The bandits would become even more powerful.

He knew he had made the right decision; he just wasn't convinced the brass would agree.

For most of the journey, he followed the main road that wound its way along the perimeter of the island. He briefly considered, and then rejected, cutting across the center of the island. While the distance would have been shorter, whatever time he would have saved might have been lost trying to find a passage through the inhospitable southern mountains that separated Cap-Verte from the rest of Beljou.

The roadway was fairly modern from the capital and along the coast as it passed the tourist resorts. But it deteriorated considerably through the southern tip of the mountains, before becoming more accessible into Cap-Verte.

Humidity had made the ground soft and Matt could tell that several vehicles had recently passed this way. One, a smaller, lighter vehicle, was probably the jeep. Another, much bigger, had left large ruts.

In a cave at the edge of the mountains, a few hours hike from the road, he had hidden a cache of supplies. He paused only long enough to change his clothes and collect some additional ammo for his Beretta. He didn't bother with any of the rations. In a day he'd be in Liberté, Madame Lucie's village, and there'd be plenty of food. Better to save it for their escape. It never occurred to him that his mission wouldn't be successful.

Just as the road cleared the mountains and began to head inland, Matt slipped through the trees to follow a little-used track he'd discovered when he was last in the area—was it only a week ago? Although it ran parallel to the road, it was well hidden and would allow him to approach Madame Lucie's village undetected.

After walking almost a whole day in complete solitude, he began to hear more and more travelers on the main road. The closer he got to the village, the busier the road became.

Of course, he remembered suddenly, it's almost Easter. When he had left, the villagers of Liberté had been preparing for their annual carnival, which coincided with the Christian observance of Easter. Hundreds of people were expected to descend on the village—the largest in the region—for the celebration. Madame Lucie had been especially busy. Liberté was the spiritual center of Cap-Verte and Madame Lucie was the spiritual center of Liberté.

Matt slipped through the dense brush to get a closer look. There was a colorful group of musicians and dancers leading a procession of about twenty people. All were singing and chanting along to the beat of a half-dozen drummers.

He checked his bearings. He was only about two hours from the village and, given the growing number of pilgrims in the area, it would probably be safer to slip in as part of the crowd rather than risk discovery in the forest.

A man nodded as Matt joined the parade while chanting and waving his arms wildly above his head. The rhythm of the drums was hypnotic, and the journey to the village passed quickly.

As the group approached Liberté, villagers ran out to greet them. In the mêlée Matt was able to break away, and he headed directly to Madame Lucie's house.

Madame Lucie's village was much different from her sister's community. There was an air of permanence here. The houses were made of wood from the abundant forest and they were sturdily built to last. The yards were well maintained, most having small vegetable gardens and a few securely penned animals. Interspersed among the residences was the occasional shop or eating establishment. They weren't marked—everyone knew where and what they were.

Although the inhabitants of Cap-Verte were fairly self-sufficient for food, they did rely on traders to bring in manufactured goods. Since the attempted coup in the north, no one had bothered making the long arduous journey, and Matt noticed some of the shop windows looked barer than they had during his last visit.

The roads through the village were wide and well planned, yet there were very few automobiles—and even fewer that still ran. In addition to the difficulties with accessibility, the damp climate ensured that any vehicle that did make it to Cap-Verte rusted out quickly.

The streets of Liberté were almost deserted and anyone Matt did see was running in the opposite direction, anxious to get to the field where the carnival was being held. Now that the musicians and dancers had arrived, the party could really begin.

Matt knocked on Madame Lucie's door.

No answer.

He knocked again. She should be there. It was still early in the day, and she would wait until dark before making her grand entrance.

He pushed gently on the door. "Madame Lucie? It's Lieutenant Wolf. Are you here?"

He stepped into the room. Sunshine streamed in from the many windows. Despite its brightness, the room smelled of stale herbs, dried earth and something else he couldn't quite place. He heard a soft sobbing sound coming from across the room and immediately tensed, feeling for his sidearm. He relaxed when he saw that it was a young girl dressed all in white. She was seated on the floor, cradling something large on her lap, and rhythmically rocking back and forth.

He approached slowly. He recognized the girl as one of the initiates Madame Lucie was preparing to enter the voodoo society. Which one? Bernice? Bernadette? Yes, it was Bernadette.

"It's all right, Bernadette. Do you remember me? Lieutenant Wolf?"

At the girl's nod he stepped closer. Suddenly a sick feeling crept into his stomach. It was Madame Lucie whom the girl was rocking. Was she dead?

Matt bent down and felt for a pulse at Madame Lucie's neck. It was strong. Then the woman gave a big shuddering sigh and Matt was overwhelmed with the smell of rum. That was the other smell! Madame Lucie was drunk.

Easily, he lifted the woman from Bernadette's lap and carried her to a bedroom. Unlike her sister, Sophie, Madame Lucie was petite. More importantly, though, Matt had never seen her drink. He closed the door softly and returned to Bernadette, who remained seated on the floor. He held out a hand to help her up.

The girl looked around the room and appeared afraid.

"Is there someone else here?" he asked, immediately alert for any unusual sounds.

"No. But the walls have ears."

"What has happened? Why are you so afraid? Why is Madame Lucie drunk?"

Bernadette stepped closer to him and lowered her voice. "The Hougan has returned."

"The Hougan?" Matt tensed. In voodoo circles, a hougan was a male priest, but when people in these parts referred to *the Hougan*, they were talking about the leader of a group of criminals. Why would his appearance at the carnival in Liberté cause such a disturbance? Madame Lucie was the mambo here and had absolute religious authority over the village.

"He arrived several days ago. He and Madame Lucie fought. He has banished her to this house."

"He has that kind of authority?" Matt was stunned.

"The Hougan is very powerful and has many followers."

Matt's mind was racing. This added a whole new dimension to his mission. Was the Hougan responsible for Julie's disappearance? That would mean his area of operation was wider than Matt had first imagined, extending at least to Port-au-Paix, maybe even the whole island. Was more going on here than a simple extortion attempt? He desperately needed to talk to Madame Lucie—alone.

"I'll stay with her until she wakes up," Matt told the girl. "The festivities have begun. You should go."

Bernadette didn't need any additional prompting. She grabbed a white satin scarf that hung on a chair and hurried out the door.

It was a couple of hours before Madame Lucie stirred. Matt used the time to rest. With the carnival underway, he knew there was little likelihood that anyone would come—especially if it was known that Madame Lucie had been banished to her own house. He was a light sleeper and awoke quickly when he heard movement in the next room.

He put on a pot of coffee and poured some water from the pitcher into the only clean glass he could find. He wished he could offer some aspirin, but he hadn't thought to bring any when he stopped at the cave. He scoured the shelves for some food—crackers would do.

The door opened slowly and he watched Madame Lucie stumble into the room. He caught her and helped her to a chair. She squinted her eyes as if the room was too bright, although the sun had almost set. Matt handed her the water and went to pour a cup of coffee.

"I am surprised to see you here, Lieutenant Wolf." Despite her state, her voice was clear and refined. She managed to retain a certain dignity that he admired.

"No more surprised than I am, Madame." He sat opposite her and meaningfully fingered the necklace Mama Sophie had given him. "I bring you greetings from your sister. She says, '*na wé sa*'."

She snorted with the same derision as her sister. "A better day? My sister is a fool. Nevertheless, Lieutenant Wolf, you have proven yourself worthy of trust. Should you need our assistance, you have only to ask."

"I thank you, Madame, and regret that I must ask for your immediate assistance in a matter of grave importance."

She slowly sipped her coffee as he described the situation. When he was done, she sat silently for a few minutes. He had to fight down the rising panic that she would refuse to help.

"I do not know anything specifically, you

understand," she began slowly. "However, there have been rumors that the home of P'tee Jay has become occupied again."

"P'tee Jay?"

Madame Lucie smiled sadly. "P'tee Jay left many years ago to seek his fortune in the city. He is said to be blessed. His entire family succumbed to a mysterious sickness, yet he survived. The house should have been destroyed, but no one will go near it. Many have seen the spirits of the dead roam the earth looking for justice. But justice for what, if it was truly an illness that took their lives?"

"Are you saying P'tee Jay killed his family?"

She shrugged her tiny shoulders. "Who would go into a house so cursed? A man who is blessed and fears not, or a man who knows there is nothing to fear?"

"Can you tell me how to get to this house, Madame?"

"Yes, I will. But it would be best if you wait until later this evening. Wait until the Hougan has begun preparing for the sacrifices he will make to Ogoun, the warrior."

Matt remained with Madame Lucie until the moon was well into its ascent across the sky. Then he thanked her for her assistance and made his way to the carnival grounds on the edge of the village.

Hundreds of people had gathered in the clearing. There were a number of makeshift tents around the perimeter, although most of the revelers would simply sleep under the stars. He raised his gaze to the threatening sky. *If* there were any stars out tonight, that is.

As he drew closer, he saw a group of initiates dancing and chanting, beckoning the spirits. There were about a dozen of them, women dressed in white dresses and wearing long white satin scarves. Bernadette, if she noticed him, gave no sign of recognition.

Matt could smell roasting meat and approached one of the enormous fire pits. A woman was cutting large chunks off of what looked like a goat, handing it to another woman who wrapped it in a bread-like shell. Neither looked up from their task as he thankfully accepted their offering. At another pit he was offered grilled plantain and beer.

Most of the people were making their way toward the center of the field. He could sense a growing anticipation in the crowd. Something was about to happen. He was curious to see the Hougan, so he joined the masses that were singing and jostling for position.

At the center rose a tall, slim man in blood-red robes, wearing a red mask. The eyes were painted black and horns shot out from the top of the head. The group stepped back from him as he raised a cylinder above his head and began chanting.

Matt felt the hairs on his neck raise. There was something familiar about the man; some movement, a turn of the head, a gesture. He couldn't put his finger on it, but he was sure he'd seen him before. He wracked his brain trying to recall everyone he'd met on his last visit to the area. He drew a blank. With an oath of frustration, he stepped a little further back in the crowd, in case the Hougan recognized *him*.

Reaching into his container, the Hougan grabbed a handful of a powdery substance and began to draw a pattern on the ground. Matt's heartbeat quickened. He was drawing a *vèvè*! Ignoring the potential danger, Matt stepped closer again and watched in fascination as the Hougan carefully drew a series of criss-crossed lines. Then he took a small amount of the powder and, one at a time, fashioned a star at the center of each diamond.

Matt backed his way through the crowd and

surreptitiously withdrew his drawing of the Oya *vèvè* from his pocket. It was impossible to tell if there was any similarity. He'd have to come back for a closer look later. But first, he had to find Julie.

****

Julie stared down at her ankle. It had more than doubled in size since she'd battled with her captors, and it throbbed excruciatingly.

She hadn't seen the masked man again, but the other two—she had dubbed them Mutt and Jeff—were constantly around and growing bolder. They would both come into the room to give her food or water—always the two of them, together. That gave Julie some satisfaction. She had proven herself a worthy opponent.

One would stand near the door with the automatic rifle trained on her while the other would bring or remove her dishes. Mutt continued to hide behind his bandana. Jeff, on the other hand, didn't seem to mind if she saw his face. Maybe he thought she wouldn't remember him—that he blended in with the other Beljouans on the island. But she'd remember him. She had committed every facet of his face, body and movement to memory.

And she'd remember Mutt, too. It was his eyes—wary, furtive. Yes, she'd remember them if—when!—she got out of here.

The last time they had come into the room, Mutt had stood guard while Jeff came very close to her. He had tried to intimidate her with threats of what he would do to her—sexual threats. She shuddered in revulsion remembering his hot breath on her cheek and the smell of cigarettes and rum on his breath. She knew it was only a matter of time until he—or the other man—built up the courage to act. She needed to rest her ankle and regain her strength so she'd be ready when they did.

She tensed as she heard the security bolt being

released. Her heart pounded furiously. The room was in total darkness, but she could see a glint of light off the barrel of the automatic as it pushed the door open. It was too late for them to be bringing her food. This could only mean trouble. She propped herself up on the bench and clutched a folded length of chain. She'd fight them to the death.

A figure stepped into the room, holding up a lantern. He slowly swung it around, the light finally resting on Julie. He looked like Matt, and for a moment Julie wasn't sure whether she was really seeing him or if the pain in her ankle was causing her to hallucinate.

He took a step towards her and she drew back for fear that at any moment he would morph into Mutt or Jeff.

"What do you want?" she said.

"I'm here to rescue you," he said.

It *was* Matt! He was here, and he was real. She giggled, giddy with relief. "Aren't you a little short for a storm trooper?" Then, seeing his confusion, she began babbling, "Sorry. My brothers were big Star Wars fans. They're a little older..." With horror she realized there were tears running down her cheeks. Could he see them? "Where are the others?"

"No others."

"What? You came alone?"

"It seemed easier that way. Look, Major, can we just get out of here?"

Julie nodded and began to sit up. The rattle of the chain caught his attention and she heard him utter an oath. He left the room and returned quickly with an axe.

"Hold still," he said just before striking the chain close to her ankle. "We'll get the rest later."

She couldn't hide her pain as her feet touched the floor. Immediately, he was at her side, shining the light on her injured ankle. He reached out a hand to examine it, but she pulled back, stifling a gasp.

"Can you walk on it?"

"I don't think so."

"Okay." He slipped the strap of the automatic over his head and slid a hand beneath her thigh to lift her up.

"Wait a second, Lieutenant. I'll take the rifle."

"With all due respect, ma'am, I don't think you're in any position to handle a rifle."

She realized with annoyance he was right. Still, she wanted a weapon.

"Fine. Give me your sidearm."

He stared at her for a moment and then, wordlessly, pulled the Beretta from his waistband and handed it to her.

She was surprised he didn't argue with her. A soldier's sidearm was very personal. The loss of her Browning was one more grudge she'd hold against the bandits.

She passed the Beretta from hand to hand, feeling for its balance. It was larger than her gun, and heavier, too. She stroked the smooth, black barrel, marveling at how remarkable it was that the surface of the gun gave off no glare from the lantern Matt was holding. It was a beautiful weapon; sexy, confident and deadly. And so totally fitting for the man who owned it, himself the epitome of sexy, confident and, judging from the absence of her captors, deadly. She removed and reapplied the safety. Finally satisfied, she slipped it into the waistband of her camouflage pants.

"Are we ready now?"

She heard the annoyance in his voice. He didn't give her time to reply before he lifted her up and placed her over his shoulder. Julie closed her eyes.

Oh no, not again! This was so humiliating.

He swung the lantern before him as they went

through another room, and left it on the table beside some playing cards and a bottle of rum. She felt him step around something, and turned her head to see the bodies of Mutt—his bandana still secured over his face—and Jeff. Their throats had been cut.

Outside, the half moon peered out from behind a cloud, providing just enough light for traveling.

With a wave of relief, Julie saw their jeep. Her relief was short-lived and panic set in as she watched it recede from view. Where was he going? The jeep was over there.

"The jeep." Julie tried pointing towards it.

"I sabotaged it on my way in."

"You what? Why would you do that?"

"We can't use it to get out of here. It's too obvious. And I didn't want them to be able to use it, either. So I poured enough dirt into the gas tank to make sure it wouldn't go anywhere."

Julie finally gave in to her tears. "How are we going to get home?" she cried. What was he thinking? He had come here with no support. She couldn't walk. It was everything she could do just to remain conscious as every movement sent spasms of agony through her ankle. And now he had sabotaged their only means of transportation.

"Trust me."

****

She awoke with the warmth of sunlight on her face. *I must be dreaming*, Julie concluded, pulling at the blanket that covered her and rolling onto her side. The searing pain woke her completely, and she struggled to sit up.

Her shackle had been removed and she wasn't on the wooden bench in her smelly prison. She was lying on a soft, comfortable bed in a bright rose-colored room. Sunlight was flooding through a window adorned with turquoise floral curtains. And she could smell fresh coffee.

A shape rose from a chair across the room and a small, delicate woman approached her.

"Good morning, Major Collins. I am Madame Lucie. This is my home. I trust you slept well." She laid a cool hand on Julie's forehead and brushed away a stray tendril of hair.

Madame Lucie? Julie recognized the name and felt a surge of jealousy race through her as she examined the petite woman. It was impossible to tell how old she was. Her ebony skin was smooth and her figure perfectly proportioned. She had deep brown eyes that glowed with compassion and a generous smile that displayed immaculate white teeth. She was stunningly beautiful.

Looking at her, Julie felt large and clumsy. "Yes, thank you. I slept very well. Where is Matt?"

"Lieutenant Wolf? He went back to the carnival to look at something. Everyone is still sleeping after last night's festivities. He should be back soon."

Madame Lucie left the room and returned a few minutes later with a steaming cup of coffee and a plate of fresh fruit.

"You must eat to regain your strength. You still have a long journey."

Julie inhaled the coffee's aroma deeply and took a sip. It was the best coffee she had ever tasted. She was just finishing the fruit when Matt returned.

"So what's the plan?" Julie asked as soon as he entered the room.

"Good morning to you, too, Major."

Julie chose to ignore the jibe and continued. "If this is Madame Lucie's village, we must be pretty far south. Without a vehicle, how are we going to get back to the compound?"

"We'll walk."

"Walk? Are you crazy! With my ankle? Do you think you're going to carry me all the way to Port-au-Paix?"

He smiled at her. "I could."

He could be so infuriating.

"With the help of Madame Lucie, I think we can fix your ankle up within a day or so," he said. "Then we'll get you some new clothes and set out along with everyone else when the carnival is over."

"You think you can fix my ankle in a few days?" she was skeptical. Then, "What carnival?"

Matt was carefully prodding Julie's ankle. She held her breath, vowing not to cry out.

"*The* carnival. Pilgrims come from all over the region for several days of drumming, dancing, sacrificing and prophesying."

"It's a voodoo thing?"

He looked up from his task and smiled. "Yeah, it's a voodoo thing." Then he took out his knife and made a long slice up the leg of her pants, exposing her calf.

She wondered if this was the same knife he had used to kill Mutt and Jeff, and then suddenly realized what he was doing.

"Hey, that's my pants. You can't do that! What am I going to wear?"

"Madame Lucie has offered us something more appropriate for our journey."

She tried to imagine how on earth she could fit into anything Madame Lucie had to wear, and decided to let it go. She was too tired to argue and in serious danger of passing out from the pain.

Madame Lucie came into the room carrying a basin that smelled horribly of noxious herbs. Maybe passing out now wouldn't be a bad idea.

Matt and Madame Lucie examined the ankle for some time. Then the woman motioned him toward the basin. He removed a long cloth strip, wrung out the excess water, and handed it to her. She took the bandage and wrapped it around the ankle. From her pocket she withdrew something small and shiny.

The charm was placed between the first bandage and a second that she was applying. Then another charm and finally, a third bandage. All the time she was working, Madame Lucie muttered under her breath. Julie couldn't understand what she was saying. The woman's face had taken on an other-worldliness and there seemed to be an aura of light around her head.

Get a grip, Jules. You're letting all this talk of voodoo get to you.

After she was finished, Madame Lucie handed her a cup. She accepted it apprehensively and sniffed the liquid. It didn't smell so bad—a bit sweet. She took a small sip and then gulped down the whole thing. Its thick syrupy texture warmed her throat and her belly.

Matt was watching her, a smile playing on his incredibly delicious lips. He nodded approvingly as she finished the drink. She was so tired...

Each time she awoke Matt was there. He would place a cool cloth on her head and give her more of the liquid to drink.

There were times when she was sure she could hear him singing softly to himself. She found his rich baritone soothing. She didn't recognize the tune or understand the words. It was peaceful, though, in that period between sleep and awakening.

Her body steamed with her dreams. They were vivid, explicit, illicit—even more than they had been at the compound. It was strange, even though she had dreamt of Matt while she was being held hostage, they hadn't been the sexually charged dreams she'd had in Port-au-Paix. Rather than exposing her body to unknown delights, he would come to her prison and rescue her—her knight in shining armor. He had fulfilled that dream, and Julie wondered if she could expect him do the same with these latest dreams.

In her rational moments she tried to counter the effect of her dreams. *Don't be a fool, Jules. You still don't know anything about this guy. He wants something from you. Why else would he come here—alone?*

Then she'd close her eyes in eager anticipation of the images of his lovemaking that would wash over her again and again.

CHAPTER 7

The fever broke, and this time when she awoke Julie felt stronger. The light coming into the room was muted. It was either dawn or dusk. She was disoriented. How long had she been sleeping?

Her skin burned hot at the memory of her dreams. Matt had been here, in the same room with her when she was dreaming, and she hadn't cared—then. Now, she wondered whether she had cried out in her sleep or given herself away. The dreams had been so... real.

She quickly looked around. She was alone. She cocked her head to listen for sounds. Everything was still, quiet, except for a distant drumming.

"Hello?" she called. "Madame Lucie?"

The door opened and the tiny, beautiful woman sailed gracefully into the room. She smiled broadly at her.

"Oh, good. You're awake. And you look much better." She felt Julie's forehead and nodded, contentedly. As she prodded the injured ankle, Julie held her breath in anticipation of pain that didn't materialize. Madame Lucie began to unwind the bandages. Her ankle felt fine.

Julie sat up and began her own examination. The swelling had gone down and there wasn't even a bruise.

"How?" she asked incredulously.

Madame Lucie smiled at her. "There is much your Western medicine can learn from the ancient ones."

Baloney! Julie refused to believe in magic. There

had to be a logical explanation for her rapid recovery. Just because she didn't know what it was, didn't mean it didn't exist. Her ankle appeared to be healed, and that was all that mattered anyway.

Madame Lucie watched Julie. If the woman knew what was going through her mind, she gave no sign of it.

"How long have I been out?" Julie asked.

"Two days. Today is Sunday."

Sunday. Matt had said that Sunday was the day of the big celebration. Tomorrow everyone would be leaving and they needed to be ready to go, too.

"Where's Lieutenant Wolf?"

"He's preparing for your journey. I told him you would be well enough to leave with the others tomorrow."

If they were leaving she'd better test whether her ankle could really bear her weight. She slid her legs over the side of the bed and started to rise. Her legs felt weak and she stumbled. Madame Lucie rushed to her side and, with strength incredible for so tiny a woman, stopped Julie from hitting the floor.

"You're still weak from lying down so much. Let me prepare you something to eat and then you can try again."

"More voodoo potions?" Julie asked, bitterly. She hated being helpless.

The woman smiled. "No. Roasted chicken and some vegetables."

"Sorry." Julie regretted her tone. Despite the potential danger, the woman had been very generous in helping them.

Matt's approach to gaining the trust of the indigenous people was obviously very successful. It was surprising that he was still only a lieutenant. But then again, most people were under the impression he used sex to accomplish his missions. Why hadn't he bothered to set the record straight?

She ate ravenously when the food arrived. She had two helpings of the chicken and vegetables. Madame Lucie seemed pleased.

Matt arrived just as Julie was getting ready to try to stand again. She hung on to his forearm and slowly raised herself from the bed, gradually putting more weight on her legs. This time they held.

"You okay?" he asked as she released his arm.

"Yes. I feel good. Strong." She took a few tentative steps. It felt so good to be able to move again. She smiled at Madame Lucie in thanks.

The drumming in the distance had become louder, and it gave Julie an idea. "I think I'd like to get some fresh air. Can we go to the carnival?"

Matt hesitated, and Julie thought he was going to refuse. Then he seemed to change his mind.

"Sure," he said. "It would be good to be seen there. That will make it easier to leave with the group tomorrow." He turned to Madame Lucie. "But we'll need some clothes for Major Collins, and a couple of masks."

While Madame Lucie went to get the required articles, Matt noticed that Julie was starting to sway a bit and helped her sit down on the bed. "I don't want you to overdo it. You'll have to let me know when you become tired."

"Yes, Dad." She sighed exaggeratedly and was rewarded with a smile.

"I may wish to be a lot of things to you, but I assure you, a father figure isn't one of them."

Before the implications of his statement fully registered, Madame Lucie returned to the room, her arms full of clothing.

Julie wondered if the woman could feel the heightened sexual tension between her and Matt. Ever discreet, she gave no indication.

"There aren't many women in the village as tall as you, Major, but I think I have been able to modify a few things to make them suitable."

"I'll leave the two of you to it," Matt said, making a quick exit.

When she emerged from the bedroom, Julie had been transformed into a native Beljouan. She wore a long, sky-blue skirt that Madame Lucie had extended by adding a panel of ruby-red fabric at the waist. An even brighter blue blouse covered the modification nicely. Julie's pale arms were hidden by a pink shawl and she wore white gloves on her hands. Madame Lucie had wrapped her head with a red and blue scarf that completely covered her neck and blonde hair. Unfortunately, the only footwear available was a pair of old brown boots that had belonged to one of Madame Lucie's husbands. They were ugly but functional. All that remained was something to cover her face.

Julie stood uncomfortably as Matt walked around her, examining her outfit from all angles.

"Excellent, Madame Lucie. But I would expect nothing less from you."

Julie fumed as Madame Lucie positively glowed from Matt's praise. "Wouldn't it be better, given my height, for me to dress as a man? I'll really stand out in this skirt."

"No, no, no," Madame Lucie replied. "You could never pass for a man here. You move all wrong."

"At carnival no one will notice your height," Matt said. "And we'll figure something out for when we leave."

He took Julie's arm and led her to a corner where Madame Lucie knelt beside a large trunk, removing an assortment of boxes. As she gingerly opened them one at time, Julie was mesmerized. Inside each was a beautifully crafted mask. There were birds and animals, and suns and stars, and a few that were just a multitude of colors and gemstones. None resembled the hideous mask of her kidnapper.

She reached out to take a large, moon-faced silver one. It was very plain and wouldn't draw any attention.

"No." Matt stopped her. "This one."

The mask he handed her was a bright iridescent blue. The face of a bird, it had a long thin yellow beak and was adorned with a variety of multi-colored feathers. It was stunningly beautiful and so delicate—everything Julie wished she was. She put it on and Matt nodded approvingly.

"Then I get to pick one for you," she said.

He waved her on good-naturedly.

She scanned the boxes and then she saw it. It was perfect. She carefully lifted it up to examine it more closely. It was the face of a wolf. Not a fearsome wolf meant to scare; this was a gentle wolf with a kind face, a long elegant snout and large openings for eyes.

As he put it over his face even Madame Lucie seemed surprised by how well it suited him.

"One more thing." Matt stopped Julie as she headed for the door. From a table he picked up a small, metallic object and held it out to her. It was a Derringer—a lady's gun!

"What am I supposed to do with that?" she asked.

"Nothing, I hope. But if you need it, it'll get the job done."

She looked at him skeptically and then, reluctantly, reached into her waistband to remove Matt's Berretta.

Their hands met as they exchanged guns. Behind the mask Julie could see his eyes darken. Was she imagining the unfulfilled passion there? Or was she transferring to him her own desire? She felt light, as if she were floating. When he took a step back and lowered his gaze to the gun, Julie crashed back to earth, but at least she could breathe again.

She examined the Derringer. It was barely larger than her palm. She checked that it was loaded and then dropped it into one of her skirt's generous pockets.

Julie followed Matt out the door. She stopped on the threshold as Madame Lucie bid them farewell.

"Aren't you coming with us?"

"I dare not. Even in costume I would be recognized."

Julie didn't understand, but with Matt urging her out of the house she didn't have time to ask questions.

****

The carnival was in full swing when they arrived. On the edge of the clearing Julie saw a group of young women dressed in white, chanting as they swayed back and forth in time with the beat of the drums. The starkness of their costumes was a contrast to the kaleidoscope of colors all around them.

"Initiates," Matt whispered to her. "They've been doing this for three days."

No wonder their eyes were glazed, she thought.

He took her arm and led her into the crowd. She needn't have worried that their height would make them stand out. Around her were people of all shapes and sizes. Some were walking on stilts, some were riding unicycles, and some were even wearing those hideous platform shoes from the seventies. Compared to most of the revelers, she and Matt looked positively common.

Her senses were overwhelmed with new sights, smells and sounds. Rum and other liquids were in abundance and fire pits were offering a multitude of delicacies. All around people were chanting and dancing, their bodies moving together and apart in unison. Great, glowing torches, sprinkled throughout the field, provided an eerie glow to the dancers. Julie found her body swaying to the hypnotic beat of the drums' rhythm.

There must be a thousand people here!

Among so many and in disguise, Julie felt anonymous. To these people she was only what she appeared to be. It was liberating, and she drank in its headiness. At home, everywhere she went people knew who she was. It had always been so. She had never been sure whether her friends and teachers had seen her for herself or as an extension of her famous family. Every success and every failure had been tinged with suspicion. Had she really deserved it? Or had she been rewarded or punished because of the Collins name?

She took Matt's hands and pulled him deeper into the crowd. She swung her hips provocatively and closed her eyes, allowing her newfound sense of freedom to wash over her.

She felt him take hold of her waist and pull her close. She wrapped her arms around his neck and leaned into him. She lay her head on his shoulder and ground her hips into his. He pulled her closer, his hands dropping to cup her bottom. She could feel him harden and thrilled to the passion she felt between her own legs.

The drums quickened and she could hear the dancers around them whirling in an ever-increasing frenzy. Yet they stayed locked together in a slow, mesmerizing waltz. She leaned even closer to him as if they could melt into one.

With a groan he pushed her away. "You're killing me, here," he said, his voice rough.

She smiled up at him. Good. Let him have a taste of how she felt when he was around. "Funny, you don't feel dead," she said, glancing down him meaningfully.

"Julie—"

Something was happening. The crowd had

worked itself up to a fevered pitch although the drumming had stopped. Still chanting and gyrating, the group was moving as one toward the center of the field. Matt and Julie were caught in the crush. He grabbed her arm so they wouldn't be separated.

"What's going on?" she asked, breathlessly trying to keep her footing.

"I think the ceremony's about to begin."

Matt and Julie remained a fair distance back. The crowd was swarming around what appeared to be a flatbed truck parked in the middle of the field.

From nowhere, the Hougan leaped onto the truck as the crowd emitted a thunderous cheer. He was dressed in the same blood-red robes and mask as when Matt had seen him earlier. He raised his arms and began an incantation.

"Oh, my God!" Julie felt weak and hung on tighter to Matt. She whispered, "That's him!"

"You know him?"

"He's the leader. The one who's responsible for my kidnapping. He came to the hut, just once, and he had a mask on—a different mask—but I'd know him anywhere."

She shivered and Matt wrapped an arm around her shoulders and pulled her closer. He didn't seem surprised by her revelation.

"You know?"

"Suspected."

"We've got to do something. We can't just let him get away with it." Julie could hear the rising panic in her own voice.

"There's nothing we can do right now," Matt said, firmly. "He's surrounded by hundreds of supporters and there are just two of us." He gave her hand a comforting squeeze. "But we'll get him, don't worry. We'll get him."

She had to fight back tears of frustration—the same frustrated helplessness she had felt while being held captive. He was so close... She lowered her hand and felt the Derringer in her pocket. A lot of good that would do. If only she had a real gun.

Matt turned her to him. Holding both her shoulders he stared into her eyes, as though willing her to trust him. "I promise you, Julie, he will pay for what he did."

She nodded. Even with the mask on, she could tell he was sincere. She took a deep breath and turned back to the Hougan.

A young man was weaving his way through the crowd, leading a goat, draped with a crimson cloth and supporting a burning candle on each of its horns. The crowd parted before them. The goat wasn't being very co-operative, and the mob began yelling insults at the unfortunate young man.

The Hougan jumped down from the truck and, despite her height, it became difficult for Julie to see him. Still, she could tell there was considerable commotion.

"What is going on?" Julie asked.

"They are preparing the goat for sacrifice. It can only be put to death after it has eaten and drunk sacred food and liquid. If it refuses, it's understood that the victim has refused death and another animal will be chosen for sacrifice."

She was tempted to draw closer, but Matt held her steady.

"As soon as the animal has eaten or drunk, it becomes the property of the *lwa*. At the same moment, the person who is to perform the sacrifice becomes possessed by the *lwa*."

Suddenly the crowd fell still and silent. Time seemed to have stopped and Julie held her breath in anticipation. Then with a terrific roar the masses burst into life again, drums beating wildly. The Hougan leapt back onto the truck and raised the body of the goat above his head. Then he jumped down again, disappearing from Julie's view.

"What *lwa* are they honoring?" Julie asked.

"Ogoun, the warrior."

"Are they preparing for battle?"

"Not necessarily. He's a traditional god for this region. Madame Lucie would have performed similar rites had she been allowed. But I think this Hougan's motives are somewhat more sinister. Ogoun is said to be the *lwa* that planted the idea for the slave revolt that resulted in their freedom one hundred and fifty years ago. Some are now calling on him to help the people attain a government more responsive to their needs. I don't think this is a call for battle as much as it is the Hougan trying to consolidate his control over the region."

"But Madame Lucie doesn't want a revolt. Surely she can calm everyone down when the festival is over."

"She'll try." He turned to Julie and smiled. "And we will help any way we can."

Matt insisted they leave the carnival. Julie needed to rest before they began their journey the next day.

As they made their way through the carnival grounds and then along the deserted streets of the village, Julie's head was spinning with images of the Hougan, the goat, and Matt.

Madame Lucie's house was quiet, seemingly deserted when they entered. In her bedroom, Julie fell back on the bed and Matt began unlacing one of her boots.

"I can do that," she said half-heartedly.

"I know."

She sighed, anticipating every movement of his hands as they slowly loosened the laces of her left boot, eyelet-by-eyelet, and then caressing her ankle and heel as he slid it off and let it drop on the floor. She shivered, expectant, as he began to do the same with the right boot.

She imagined him moving his fingers under her skirt and up her thighs to caress the curve of her hips.

She heard the second boot drop to the floor and felt a rush of cool empty air as Matt took a step back and gazed down at her.

Julie propped herself up on one elbow fighting disappointment. “Is that it?”

The wolf's face continued to look down at her, its large, dark eyes questioning. She smiled under her own mask and reached for him. The anonymity was arousing.

He paused momentarily and then took her hand and came to the bed.

She rolled onto her back and closed her eyes. She felt the bed move. Then his hands were unbuttoning her blouse. Slowly. Painstakingly slow. She felt him part the fabric, exposing her bare skin.

Heat surged through her. She felt as if she was on fire. She wanted to feel his skin and began to unbutton his shirt. She wanted to be as maddeningly slow as he had been, but she was too impatient.

He chuckled softly. As though recognizing her dilemma, he stopped her hands and began the job himself. Slowly. Deliberately. Button-by-button. He was stripping for her! She wanted him to hurry, but she didn't want it to end. She hadn't realized she was holding her breath until he finally shrugged off his shirt, and she gasped at the sight of his broad chest. She raised her hand and, with her fingertips, traced the line of dark hair that ran down to his belly.

Then her hands circled behind him and she grabbed his buttocks, reveling in the firmness through the cotton fabric. His hips arched towards her and she could see his erection straining to be free.

She heard his sharp intake of breath and felt his stomach quiver as she slid her fingers along the waistband from his back to the front of his pants. She began to fumble with the button. Finally successful, she began to unzip them.

His hands stilled hers and she thought he was going to take over. But then he stood up and quickly left the room.

She barely had time to register what had happened—that he had left—when he was back again, closing the door softly behind him. In two quick paces he returned to the bed, dropping a handful of colorful small packages beside her.

Condoms!

Julie was stunned. How could she have forgotten about condoms? Every soldier was issued them. Julie usually kept some on her, not for her own use, but in case one of her men—or women—needed one. But of course the Hougan and his bandits had taken them along with everything else.

Gratitude flooded through her. Thank goodness he still had some of his wits about him. "Thank you," she whispered.

He bowed his head in acknowledgement and knelt on the bed beside her.

The wolf's eyes never left the bird's as he undid her bra and pushed it out of the way. It was the only part of his face she could see. They told her everything she needed to know.

His breath was warm on her breasts. "Julie," he moaned as he circled one nipple with a fingertip and then clasping it, gently tugged. He fully cupped her other breast and began stroking the nipple between his fingers. The sensation was electric, shooting out from her breasts and engulfing the rest of her body.

Julie returned to the zipper of Matt's pants and urged them over his hips. Her long fingers wrapped around the enormous phallus, which rose to meet her. She sighed contentedly. Her dreams hadn't elaborated on her memories of their first night together. Slowly, she caressed Matt, her thumb rubbing softly over the tip of his swollen member, her hand clenching a rhythm of want and need.

She desperately wanted to taste him. She could recall the salty sweetness of his skin, the firmness of his lips and the insistent pressure of his tongue. But there would be no lips or teeth or tongues tonight. It was an excruciatingly pleasurable pain. She barely knew where she was anymore. Her gaze remained fixed on Matt's unnatural face. Her entire consciousness was filled with this strange creature.

As Julie continued her ministrations, she could feel the heat from her own moisture running between her legs. Finally, she couldn't wait any longer. She needed to feel him inside of her. She reached for one of the packages and with fumbling fingers managed to release the latex jacket and roll it down over Matt's penis. She lay back and, pushing her stockings down she raised her skirt and hungrily pulled him onto her hips.

He positioned himself above her and drove into her in a single thrust, then partially withdrew and thrust again. Her hands grasped his buttocks as she urged him deeper and deeper. She could feel every inch of him driving into her and she arched her body, eager to receive him.

Her passion rising, she was being driven to the edge. On and on it went. He wouldn't let up. Teasing. Coaxing. Whispering her name over and over. "Julie... Julie... Julie..."

****

Matt stared down at Julie. He had taken off his own mask, but didn't dare remove hers.

Well now you've done it, Boyo. No matter how he tried to wrap it up in a sense of responsibility for her or admiration of her strength of character, he had to face the truth. He had fallen in love.

He rose from the bed and covered her with a sheet. Then he crossed the room to the chair he'd claimed when she was fevered.

When had it happened? He was so certain he had his emotions under control. And the worst of it was he was sure she felt the same way about him but could never admit it.

She risked disciplinary action if word of their affair ever got out. The shame would probably kill her. It would certainly kill her career and, for Julie, that was the same as death.

It was unfair. While she would be pilloried from all sides, the very same people that would condemn him in public would privately congratulate him. It fit perfectly with the reputation he had developed for himself. And that would only make it worse for her—another woman fallen victim to his charm. He cringed at the thought of the derision she would face.

Still, if there was a way—any way—to make it work...

What? What would you do, Boyo? What would you be prepared to give up?

Everything!

The answer startled and scared him.

She gave a shuddering sigh and rolled on her side. He wondered if she was dreaming of him and waited to see if she would cry out his name as she had done before. She'd be mortified if she knew.

He smiled, remembering how his body responded the first time she'd done it. It stirred again, now, at the thought that he may be the subject of her dream.

He wanted to go to her and take her again. This time without secrets, without masks. Just the two of them—honest and real. He actually rose and stood beside her bed. No. As much as he wanted her, he'd let her sleep.

Julie's mask shifted to reveal the curve of one

cheek. He stroked it and was rewarded with a sigh of contentment. She'd been surprised at his choice of mask for her, but pleasantly so. How could he tell her that was how he saw her? A delicate, gentle soul beneath an exterior of tempered steel. Far too beautiful to be earthbound, she deserved to soar above this world.

He was pleased by her choice of mask for him. It wasn't just that it was a wolf. There were several wolves she could have chosen. This particular wolf seemed to encompass everything his grandparents had told him about his clan. Without warning, he heard his grandfather: *While we might explore on our own, we prefer the company of others.*

Suddenly the loneness he sought seemed more of a burden than a relief. What would it be like to share a life with someone you loved—a love like he had seen between his grandparents?

Whoa! Stop right there. He didn't dare go down that path. No, he needed to get Julie back to safety—it was his fault she was in danger—finish the mission, and then get as far away from her as he could. For both their sakes.

He began pacing in frustration. He needed to get out of here. The room was stifling.

As he stepped into the sitting room, Madame Lucie rose from a chair.

"I've been waiting to talk with you."

Matt felt the hairs on his neck stand up. She motioned for him to sit beside her on the small sofa where they could whisper. Something was definitely wrong.

"They know she's missing," Madame Lucie began without preamble. "They do not know how she escaped, only that she did and several men are dead."

"They're looking for her, then. Are they looking for her alone or do they think she's with someone?"

She shrugged. "I don't think they know of your involvement. But they are most definitely looking for her. They searched every house in the village this evening while everyone was at carnival."

"Here, too? Are you all right?"

He could see a small smile touch her lips.

"I am fine," she said. "They may follow the dark one, but they would not dare disrespect me. I allowed them to come and look into each room, but they were not allowed to go through any of my belongings. After they left, I burned the Major's uniform and everything else I could find that would show that you were here. Everything except for this."

Madame Lucie crossed the room and pulled a large object from behind a table. She turned to show the automatic M-16 rifle he had taken from the kidnappers. It was almost as big as she was.

"This I will keep as a replacement for my Derringer."

Matt couldn't stop himself from laughing out loud. The image of tiny Madame Lucie wandering around with the automatic was too ludicrous to contemplate. Still, the rifle was far too big to take with them, and Julie needed a firearm. It would have to be the Derringer, although he was fairly certain she'd find a way to take the rifle if given the chance.

Madame Lucie chuckled, also, as she put the automatic back in its hiding spot. "I think we will keep this out of sight until your Major has left," she said, reading his mind.

He turned to Madame Lucie as she took her seat beside him, again. He had a lot of questions he needed answered. He wasn't sure she could help him with them all, but there was one above all others that he needed to ask her.

"Madame Lucie, your sister is a mambo, like you.

This is an area rich in your religion, with many faithful. There would be room for two of you, would there not?"

Madame Lucie's eyes shone with unshed tears. "It was our mother's wish that the two of us lead the faithful together. It was how she trained us. We were never meant to serve alone."

"Why did Mama Sophie leave?"

"She fell in love with a boy and followed him to the city."

"Was he a hougan?"

"No. Not then."

CHAPTER 8

Julie opened her eyes. It was cold. It was dark. Matt, of course, was nowhere to be seen. She was miserable.

Madame Lucie slipped quietly into the room. She brought with her a basin of warm water and a cup of strong coffee. Julie wanted to ask if she knew where Matt was, but was too embarrassed.

After the woman left, she rose slowly from the bed, stripped off her remaining clothing and began to wash.

Mesmerized by the long rivers of warm water flowing down her naked body to the earthen ground, she allowed herself to be transported back to the previous night. Had it been real? It was so hard to tell. Matt seemed always to fill her nights.

The door opened and she started.

Matt?

Madame Lucie walked into the room with an armful of clothes and she relaxed.

"There is no time to wash what you wore yesterday so you may use these," she said.

Julie looked at the skirt, blouse, and jacket the woman laid on the bed. They were even uglier than the other clothes—if that was possible.

"The boots, I'm afraid, will have to do." Madame Lucie motioned to the brown work boots lying askew on the floor.

She winced remembering how uncomfortable they were. *Oh, well, beggars can't be choosers.* "Thank you. They're fine. I appreciate all you've—"

Madame Lucie waved her hand dismissively as

she left the room.

Julie dressed quickly, remembering to transfer the tiny Derringer into the pocket of her new skirt. Then she made the bed—deliberately avoiding any memories of what had taken place there last night—and carefully folded the soiled clothes, placing them in a neat pile on a chair in the corner.

As she entered the main room her eyes were immediately drawn to the large ceramic bowl, overflowing with small colorful packets, that sat on top of an ornately carved wooden credenza.

Absently, she ran her hands over her hips, smoothing the pocket where she had placed the leftover condoms from the night before. Why hadn't she noticed the bowl before? It made sense, though. Madame Lucie was not only the spiritual head of the community, she was responsible for the physical well-being of her people, too.

Matt was examining a document on a table littered with small packages wrapped in a brown paper. Without looking up, he motioned her to join him.

Annoyed at his presumption that he could order her around, she ignored him and went to the stove where Madame Lucie was stirring a big pot of some sort of mashed root vegetable.

"Breakfast?" Julie asked dubiously.

"Plantain and sugar cane."

"Umm, yummy."

Madame Lucie snorted. "It will give you strength for your journey. I've also gathered some food you may take with you. Water," she paused meaningfully, cocking her ear to the din of the rain hitting on the tin roof, "that shouldn't be a problem."

Julie smiled. She liked Madame Lucie more and more. She turned to see Matt watching her, his face unreadable.

"Good morning," she said brightly, hoping it

would annoy him. He didn't react.

"No, it's not going to work," he said, ignoring Julie and speaking directly to Madame Lucie. "Fooling a bunch of revelers is one thing, but she won't have a mask on today. And now that they know she's missing—"

"They know I'm missing?" Julie went cold. "I suppose it wouldn't take too long for them to figure it out. I mean, once the Hougan finished his ceremony he probably wanted to check on his minions."

"He knew before the ceremony," he said.

She looked from Matt to Madame Lucie. *He knew before the ceremony? She was at the ceremony. What if he had discovered her?*

"You were well-disguised and there were a lot people there," he said, reading her thoughts. "He searched the village, though. Madame Lucie burned all your things to make sure they wouldn't be found."

"Everything?" With nothing of her own she felt vulnerable.

"Yes, I'm afraid so, Major. I am most sorry," Madame Lucie lowered her eyes.

She immediately regretted her reaction. The woman had done so much to help them, at great personal risk to herself. More risk, apparently, than Julie had contemplated.

She could feel Matt and Madame Lucie's gazes on her. "It's fine," she said quickly. "I appreciate your quick thinking, and all you've done for us."

Matt rose from the table and walked towards her. Her heart raced as he drew closer, and she forced herself to remain still as he peered into her face. Sparks shot up her arm as he lifted one of her hands.

"We've got to darken her skin somehow. Her hair we wrap, but her skin..."

"I'll brew up some tea. With this rain it won't last too long, though—hopefully, long enough to get you safely to the mountains," Madame Lucie said.

"Good but we have to be quick about it. I can hear movement outside."

****

The rains had begun in earnest overnight. The hint of dampness that had permeated her clothes and sheathed her skin with clamminess over the past few days now threatened to overwhelm her in a relentless barrage of water. Julie sank deeper into the oversized clothing, fearful that the water would wash away the tea Madame Lucie had used to stain her skin a few shades darker.

She and Matt had slipped easily into the throng of pilgrims exiting Liberté. He told people she was his old auntie, "quite out of her mind." He claimed this would keep people away, but she thought he seemed just a little too pleased with the ruse. Still, it seemed to work. No one approached her as she uncomfortably hunched over to mask her height, and muttered curses to Matt and the rain under her breath.

It wasn't a problem to appear to have difficulty walking. The flatbed truck from the night before lumbered along the track, leaving deep, muddy ruts in its wake. It made each step in her too-large boots a battle with the sucking mud. The air was filled with the smell of decay and diesel.

It was a slow, somber procession. Many in the group were obviously suffering the ill effects of three days of revelry. Some climbed onto the back of the truck and, every so often, someone would stop by the side of the road to vomit. Only the children seemed unaffected. They ran back and forth, alternately urging their beleaguered parents to move faster and seeking food.

Throughout the morning, Matt and Julie slowly fell further and further back in the crowd. Finally, Matt paused to allow the last of the procession to pass. He appeared to be adjusting the sack he had taken from Madame Lucie while he scanned in all directions.

Julie's body tensed. This was it. They were making their escape!

While Julie's heart raced in anticipation, it was, in the end, rather anti-climactic. She and Matt merely slipped unnoticed through the trees and began following a trail that seemed to run parallel to the main road. Periodically, she'd hear voices from the crowd off to her right.

Although it was a relief to be able to walk upright again, the going was still slow. The path was narrow and not well defined. In fact, there were times when she was sure they had lost it totally. Matt didn't slow his pace. He seemed to know where he was going, and she was determined to keep up.

He hadn't spoken directly to her since they left Madame Lucie's village. The narrow path forced them to walk single file. They couldn't possibly hold a conversation. And even if they could, they were still too close to the road to be sure their voices wouldn't carry. Yet, as she stared at his back, trying not to focus on how it tapered from broad shoulders to a narrow waist, she found herself willing him to turn to talk to her—to acknowledge her presence. She knew she was being ridiculous.

What do you expect him to say? she chided herself.

Anything!

Julie didn't know why his silence bothered her. She had been so disappointed when she awoke this morning to find him gone from her bed, but she wasn't prepared to talk about what had happened between them.

Just what did happen, Jules?

She sighed deeply, and briefly closed her eyes. It was a mistake and she stumbled, letting out a cry of alarm.

He turned to steady her. His touch was fire to her skin and she pulled back.

"I'm fine," she said curtly.

He held a finger to his lips and nodded toward the road. Then he continued without further comment.

Get a grip! You're not some foolish schoolgirl. You're a military officer—his commander—and you're in hostile territory. She fingered the Derringer, hidden in the deep pocket of her skirt. *With a toy gun for protection.*

Yet, with her eyes on Matt, it was difficult not to think about last night. Her heart raced, and despite the cooling rain she felt a heat spread between her thighs.

What had she been thinking when she had come on to him? Well she *hadn't* been thinking, and that was all there was to it. Maybe it was the potential danger of their situation that so aroused her. The adrenalin from battle he had told her about. Or perhaps she had been bewitched by the rhythms of the festival, its smells and mood—mysterious and sensual.

Whatever the cause, she had been the one to initiate things. He certainly hadn't objected, she noted. But what had he been thinking? Was he attracted to her? Since arriving in Beljou he had behaved as a perfect gentleman, if not a perfect subordinate officer.

Julie gasped. He was a subordinate officer. Her subordinate! What if he had slept with her because he felt obligated to obey her?

She tried to dismiss the thought as ridiculous. He was hardly the type of man who would obey that kind of order. Besides, he had slept with her before... He had known who she was then, too. She was the one who had been ignorant.

She felt bile rise in her throat. It was always the same. She could never be sure whether people wanted to be with her or what she represented. Matt was no different.

Instead of hardening her, the thought sent a wave of longing so intense it sucked all the air out of her lungs. Tears filled her eyes, blinding her so she didn't notice that Matt had stopped, until she walked into him.

"Sorry," she gulped. "Rain in my eyes."

His hands were on her arms, steadying her. His eyes held a strange look as he gazed into her upturned face. He was so close she could taste his scent as his breath warmed her skin. For a second she thought he was going to kiss her, and she swayed closer in anticipation. Just in time, she took hold of her emotions and stepped back.

"Did you say something?" She forced her gaze away.

"I asked if you wanted to stop for a bit. It'll take us most of the day to get to the edge of the mountains. There's a cave there, where I've put some supplies."

Julie knew he was good at his job, but couldn't help but be impressed.

"Really? Supplies?"

"Well, we're not talking champagne and caviar," he said. "Just a few staples. Mostly, it will be a chance to get out of the rain and have some hot food before we make our final push back to base."

Julie cursed her traitorous heart. How dare it flip at the sight of his smile? The thought of food and shelter, however, lightened her mood considerably.

They moved off the path to the relative shelter of a tall tree.

"What about the others?" she motioned toward the main road.

"The road goes through all of the local villages

and most will be home by the end of today. It then follows along the perimeter of the island, eventually arriving at Port-au-Paix. This path is good for another day or so, and then we'll have to rejoin the main road to get through the mountains. It'll probably take us a couple of days to get back to the base."

"But on the road we'll be more exposed, won't we?"

"Yeah, but once we're out of Cap-Verte the people are less superstitious. The Hougan won't have as much support. In fact, by tomorrow night we can probably count on a warm bed and be able to contact the base to tell them where we are."

Julie imagined sinking into a warm bath. "How do you know all this? And how did you find this path? I mean you weren't here for very long before you came back to the compound—just a few weeks?" She was annoyed that she couldn't keep a note of admiration out of her voice.

Matt shrugged. "I don't know. It's what I do. This track was probably made by the bandits to allow them to get into and out of Cap-Verte quickly and easily. They probably know a way through the mountains, too, but I haven't had time to figure that out."

"There's no danger that we'll run into... anyone?" Julie said, thinking of the Hougan. She hadn't seen him in the crowd leaving Liberté.

"No. The Hougan left in the middle of the night," Matt said, once again displaying his annoying mind-reading trick. "He took a vehicle and will have to stick to the main road. No one has been along here since I took it a few days ago. And we're not being followed."

"How do you know?"

"I just do."

That statement from anyone else would have

sounded boastful. Matt stated it so matter-of-factly that Julie found herself unable to raise an objection to his arrogance.

Although she was anxious to be out of the rain, the growling of her stomach told Julie she should attend to more immediate concerns.

She rummaged in the pockets of her overlarge skirt while Matt opened his sack and withdrew an earthenware container. He opened the lid and Julie immediately smelled the spicy, pungent aroma of cooked meat.

"We'll have to eat it cold," he said. "I'm not sure I could get a fire started even if I could find something dry to use as kindling."

She shrugged, pushing away the images of last night—bountiful amounts of succulent meat roasting over fire pits, swaying to the hypnotic rhythms of drums, eyes dark with passion peering from the face of a wolf, making love to...

She pulled a couple of bananas out of her pockets. Although they looked like they'd seen better days, she held them up triumphantly and declared: "A feast!"

They ate in silence. Determined to put thoughts of the previous evening out of her mind, she began making a mental checklist of what she'd have to do when she returned to base. There would have to be a debriefing, and she would have to answer a lot of questions about how she had been abducted and what had happened. Matt would have to describe his role...

Suddenly, she turned to him. "Why didn't you tell anyone where I was before you came to get me? Why did you come alone?"

Julie saw his shoulders sag before he took a deep breath, preparing himself to respond. So, he'd been expecting the question.

"Can we just say that I felt responsible?"

"That doesn't do it. You are one person, alone, against who knows how many bandits. They'd captured a commanding officer. It makes no sense. Why would you risk two lives just to play the hero?"

He winced at the word 'hero' and bit out a retort, "I thought you knew me better. I have no interest in personal heroics."

"I don't really know you at all!" Julie was surprised at how much that statement hurt her. On the one hand, he seemed the epitome of the stereotypical macho male; but on the other, he had displayed a sensitivity and compassion for the people of Beljou that she found disarming.

"I thought I'd made it perfectly clear in my report. This whole region is a powder keg. Sure, we've subdued the opposition and have brought a measure of political stability back to Beljou, but there is a greater danger. There are many factions in this country. Not everyone is happy to see America here. They don't all buy our dream of democracy. Men like the Hougan want to advance their own personal agendas—they can't do that if we're here and able to help bring up the standard of living for the average person. They'll do whatever they can to cause dissent." His tone softened. "If I had returned to the compound and told them what happened—that the commanding officer, the daughter of the Army Chief of Staff no less, had been kidnapped by bandits—what do you think they would have done?"

She remained silent. She was beginning to understand his concerns.

"The response would not have been measured," he continued. "There would have been an immediate mobilization of troops into this area. Every Beljouan would have been questioned. Houses searched. It wouldn't have mattered that the people of Cap-Verte were innocent of this—that it was the work of a few bandits. They would *all* have paid the price. And in the end, so would we.

"A military response is exactly what the Hougan was hoping for. It would play perfectly into his plan. He could then raise the country up against America and Beljou's current government. And, when the time was right, you would most certainly have been killed, just to up the ante."

She felt a shiver run down her spine. She sensed he was right, but she couldn't condone his lack of confidence in the American military. It was too deeply ingrained in her.

"You don't have a lot of respect for our military, do you?" she asked. "I can't help wondering what you're doing here, if you think we're doing more harm than good."

"I never said that," he snapped. "I just think we sometimes act without fully weighing all our options. Subtlety can sometimes be more effective than force."

"You took a big chance, risking our lives like this. What if you'd been captured or killed before you got to me? What if Madame Lucie had been working with the Hougan?"

"I know it was a risk. But I did arrange for information about your whereabouts to be given to Master Sergeant Murray. I think by now they know, generally, where you were taken and are probably mobilizing their response."

Julie didn't know what to say. Of course he would have had an alternate plan. He was a professional and very good at what he did. Not only did everyone say so, she had seen it herself. To cover her discomfort she went on the attack.

"I don't get you. You show very little respect for the chain of command. You balk at authority. And yet, you chose to be a soldier."

Matt chuckled. "Yeah, I don't think my guidance counselor would have foreseen it, either. But my mother wanted me to go to college. I wanted to go to college. We couldn't afford it, so going on the government's ticket seemed the only solution. I was a good student but not good enough to qualify for a scholarship. The thing is, if we'd stayed on the reservation, my tuition would have been covered." He paused, then shook his head and continued, an edge of bitterness creeping into his voice. "Anyway, after college I did my stint and when that was over I just stayed on. I didn't know what else I'd do. My skills are somewhat—ah—specialized, I guess you'd say. Not much use outside of the military—certainly not when they're being offered by an Indian."

Julie started. "You don't think you'd be discriminated against because of your heritage, do you?"

Matt snorted.

"No, really," she persisted.

"I've been in the military since I was eighteen. I have been decorated and received commendations, and yet I remain a lieutenant. Wilkes, twelve years my junior with not even a fraction of my experience, was promoted ahead of me. Draw your own conclusion."

Julie paused. She, of all people, knew the inequalities of the military, but in this case she was quite certain Matt's lack of promotion had more to do with his reputation than his background. And yet...

"I'm not really complaining," he said quickly. "Especially now with this new re-con duty. I can keep to myself, do my own thing—sort of. How can I be unsatisfied with all that I have, when the people here are able to keep hope despite everything they've been through? It's only when I go back to the compound and get sucked into all that political crap that it bugs me."

Julie didn't know how to respond. She couldn't

disagree, and yet to agree seemed to invalidate everything she had fought so hard to achieve. Her whole life had been "that political crap." It still was. She didn't necessarily like it, either. That was just the way it was.

It was ironic, she thought. Matt had created a mask to hide from others who he really was, while her greatest wish was for others to look past her family legacy to see her for herself.

"I think we should get going." She stood up.

He nodded, hoisted the sack on his back and headed back to the trail without looking back.

Relieved that the narrowness of the path forestalled further conversation, she fell into step behind him.

****

The cave comfortably fit two people and their gear. The small opening, through which they were obliged to crawl, opened into a larger cavern, perhaps ten feet square. At the center there was just enough headroom for one of them to stand. A lantern had been hung there to illuminate as much of the cave as possible. Although dry inside, the dampness of the air hung on the rocks, and the rain continued to pelt down outside.

Near the opening, Matt lit a small single-burner stove and boiled some water. Into the pot he added a couple of chocolate bars he kept as part of his emergency stash. Sometimes only chocolate would do—even soggy chocolate.

Julie hadn't spoken to him since they'd stopped for lunch, and he was afraid he'd told her too much about his feelings for the military.

He looked over to her. She was sitting on the floor, leaning against the wall, arms wrapped tightly around herself, eyes closed.

"You need to get out of those clothes," he said.

Slowly, she opened her eyes and gave him a

quizzical look.

"You'll freeze," he added quickly, trying to dispel the image of her partially naked body, sensuous and warm, reaching out to him from Madame Lucie's bed. "Here." He tossed her a blanket and turned his back, determinedly stirring the chocolate in the pot.

He could hear a rustle of fabric as she removed the clothes and then the thwap of wet material being laid out on the rocks by the fire.

Matt stared at the impossibly large skirt, again contemplating the smooth skin it had covered.

He turned to look at Julie. She had returned to her position by the wall, the blanket wrapped closely around her. Her lips had a bluish tinge and he resisted the desperate urge to warm them with his own.

Just stop it, Boyo!

He had come close to kissing her in the forest. Too close. He needed to stay away from her. Just get her back to base as soon as possible, and then get the hell out of there.

It was good that she wasn't talking to him, his head tried to reason with him. It was good that he had disappointed her. And while he knew he needed to stay away from her for her own sake, a part of him ached to make her understand. It wasn't that he didn't respect the military or like his job; he just thought it could be so much more.

Unquestioning loyalty to leaders was essential in battle, but a top-down authoritarian approach wasn't always effective for stabilization and restoration operations. He loved the people he met doing this work. He wanted to help them, but felt they needed to play a greater role in finding their own solutions—even if those solutions diverged from America's idea of what *it* wanted.

If only he could make her understand. No, it wasn't important that she understand. Given her background, she probably never could. *Just as well. Keep her distant.*

"I knew your brother, you know." He was surprised to hear his own voice. Despite his best intentions he was unable to ignore her.

"What?" She opened her eyes.

He poured the steaming chocolate into a cup—he had only one in his mess kit—and brought it over, sliding down the wall beside her.

"Your brother, Richard. I served under him in Serbia. He was a lieutenant colonel then. We all thought he was great."

Julie sighed, sat up straighter, and turned her gaze onto him.

"He is great," she said, resigned. "Both he and Stephen are great."

He didn't know what made him push her further. He knew she was hung up on her family. She needed to get over it. Wet, exhausted, and hiding in a cave, this probably wasn't the best time. She was probably still nursing her injured pride after being abducted and questioning her ability to lead. No, he amended; maybe this was the best time. What more did she have to lose?

"I don't know Stephen, but all the men were thrilled when Dick made colonel. Quite a feat at his age—for both of them, I guess."

"You're not going to start on family connections and whether they had help, are you? I'm sick of the speculation and—"

"Whoa!" He held up a hand to halt the tirade she was unleashing at him. "Didn't I just say we were happy for him? Of course he did it on his own merit. Anyone who says otherwise is just sore—nursing a personal grudge or something."

"A grudge like yours? Someone who thought he should have been promoted and wasn't?"

Matt was taken aback. How had this turned on

him? "I don't have a grudge," he said slowly.

"Sorry," she said, looking thoroughly miserable. "It's just whenever my family comes up I feel like such a failure."

"A failure?" He was truly incredulous. "How can you be a failure? Look at you! You're a major, heading a full company on a foreign mission."

"At my age my brothers were already lieutenant colonels."

"Yeah, and they're part of the fighting regiments, right? Our work is civil affairs—not nearly as glamorous or sexy as pitched battles and dogfights. We come after and try to clean up the mess—put it all back together."

"Sometimes I think it's my name that's holding me back. Not my father specifically, of course, although he never wanted me to join the military, but the whole military establishment."

"You think that some poor commander thinks that by denying you a promotion he'll somehow score points with your father?"

"You make it sound ridiculous."

"It is ridiculous. You agree that your brothers got where they are without interference, but that somehow your aspirations have been thwarted by—"

"All right!" she yelled. "But it's no more ridiculous than thinking you've been passed over because you're a Native American, and failing to consider that this Casanova, one-man-army persona you've created for yourself has something to do with it. That's not exactly command material, Lieutenant."

"Point taken, Major." He smiled inwardly, feeling that they had come to some sort of agreement—that she wasn't disappointed in him anymore. That was good, he thought. He needed to ensure they keep emotionally separated—physically, too, if last night was any indication—but they could still be friends.

Friends? Is that what you call it, Boyo? She's your C.O., and don't you forget it.

"Is it because of Dick that you knew who I was in Fayetteville?"

"Huh?" Startled, Matt stared at her uncomprehending.

"Of course it was," she said. "It's not fair that you know so much about me, and I know virtually nothing about you."

Unable to think of a way to respond that would satisfy her, he shrugged and remained silent.

"Why so secretive?" she persisted.

"I'm not being secretive. Maybe there's just nothing to talk about."

"Why don't you let me be the judge of that?" she said. "Let's play twenty questions."

"Twenty questions?"

"You know? I have twenty questions to get what information I want from you."

"Sounds more like an interrogation," he muttered.

Somehow she had the ability to turn every conversation back onto him. It would be a long trip back to base, and she was nothing if not persistent. Maybe he should just give in now. *Go ahead, tell her the truth, Boyo, and let the chips fall where they may!*

"Is it reciprocal?" he asked. "Do I get to ask you twenty questions afterwards?"

"Of course."

He nodded, amused by the sparkle he could see in her eye. "Ask away."

"And you promise to tell the truth?"

"Yes. That's one."

"Hey, that's not fair!" She was indignant.

"Next?" He ignored her protest.

"Do you have any brothers or sisters?"

"No for brothers, no for sisters. Is that two

more?" He was enjoying this.

"That was one question. Don't be smart, Lieutenant."

"Yes, ma'am."

Julie eyed him. "Aunts, uncles, cousins, grandparents?" she said quickly.

"I think you're cheating, now. There has to be a limit to how many people you can cram into a single question."

"Okay, let me rephrase. Aside from your mother—and this isn't yes or no, it's an essay question—who were the people most influential in your life, growing up?"

"After my mother left the reservation, she still allowed me to go back and visit my grandparents—her parents."

"She never went back?"

"No."

"You said before you don't know why she left. Did you ever ask her?"

"Of course, but you'd have to know my mother. She was very strong-willed. She had to be. We were the only Indians in our neighborhood. She held down two jobs just to make a life for us. She wanted the best for the two of us. But she was stubborn. Whatever made her want to leave her home and her family hardened her."

"You must have had friends growing up. A best friend?"

Matt leaned back and considered his answer carefully. "When I was young, I had lots of friends—neighborhood kids. I guess I was about twelve or thirteen when suddenly my childhood friends wouldn't play with me anymore."

"Because you were a Native American?"

"Because I was an Indian."

"I'm so sorry. What did you do?"

He shrugged. "I worked hard in school. I excelled

in sports. Nobody wanted to be my friend, but they all wanted me on their team."

"Didn't you feel used?"

"I wanted to fit in."

"What about a girlfriend? Your first kiss?"

"Laura Ritter. I think that was the hardest to take," Matt closed his eyes, surprised by the ache he still felt in his chest. "She was my first kiss. I think we were, maybe, six? I was going to marry her and live happily ever after. But..." his voice trailed off remembering his mother's words when he confided in her his feelings towards Laura, and her rejection. *Blonde-hair, blue-eyes is not for you, Boyo*, she had said. *You will never be part of their world, but you must live in it.*

"I'm sorry," Julie said softly.

He turned to her. She was staring at him with something in her eyes—pity? He gave himself a mental shake. He didn't need anyone's pity. He had not only learned how to fit in, he had made an art of it. Capable and charismatic, men found him a "good guy to have around" and women were attracted to his exotic good looks and the respectful way he treated them. Yet he could never shake the feeling that he was seen as a novelty, a token, and so his relationships were no more than skin-deep. He craved solitude, the ability to get away and just be himself. Loneliness had become a way of life for him and he liked it that way—at least until he met Julie.

"I don't need you or anyone to feel sorry for me. That's life. You learn to make the best, and I think I'm doing just fine, thank you."

"Is that why you always volunteer for the most remote assignments?" she asked after a long pause.

"Maybe I just find it easier to be alone."

"That's so sad."

OH-tuh, more of that pity! "Like I said before, I like the people I meet on my missions, and the longer

I can stay away from the political crap that goes on back at base, the better."

"When I was recovering at Madame Lucie's, you were singing. I couldn't understand the words. What language were you using and what did it mean?"

"Oh, you heard that, did you? I don't know what the words mean. When I used to visit the reservation, none of my cousins would play with me. I don't blame them. I had nothing in common with them. I didn't know their games. They didn't know mine. So I spent all my time with my grandparents. My grandmother would sing me that song at night to help me fall asleep. I don't know the exact translation, but it calls on the Great Spirit to keep watch and protect a loved one."

"And you sang it for me?"

Careful, Boyo. "I figured it couldn't hurt."

"Did your grandparents teach you a lot about your heritage?"

"Some. But they died when I was ten. First my grandfather, and then my grandmother. Within just a few weeks of one another."

"You said your mother never went back. Surely she went to their funerals."

"She said her own prayers."

"What does she think of your military career?"

"She was proud to see me get through college and take up my commission, but died shortly afterwards. Hit-and-run, by a drunk driver."

"I'm sorry. Is that why you never take leave? I heard that from Captain Wilkes."

"Where would I go on leave? I have no home. No family."

Julie remained silent for several moments. Matt was regretting that he had agreed to the game. It was bringing back too many hurtful memories. Memories he thought were deeply buried.

Suddenly she spoke. "Why did you really kiss me

when we were running from the snipers?"

Her question caught him off guard and he responded without fully considering his answer. "To stop you from asking personal questions."

"Really? Then why aren't you kissing me now?"

"I'm thinking about it." Matt leaned towards her.

She held up her hand to stop his advance. "I still have another question."

"Okay. By my count, this is it."

"Why didn't you tell me who you were when we met in Fayetteville?"

He could have kicked himself for not seeing this coming. He should have known where all this was leading. Instead, he had allowed himself to believe her twenty questions would be nothing more than a background check, an exploration of his personal past.

"Was it a kick to sleep with your commanding officer?" she persisted. "The *daughter* of the Army Chief of Staff. Did you and your friends have a good laugh?"

"No!" The word ripped out of his mouth. He turned and grabbed her shoulders harshly. "I'd never do that to you. I told no one."

"Then why?"

He released Julie and put his head in his hands. "I don't know," he said very quietly. "I recognized you when you arrived. I couldn't take my eyes off of you. Even when I wasn't looking at you, I could feel you."

"Go on," she prompted when he paused.

He raised his head, a giant shudder wracked his body and he exhaled deeply before looking into her eyes—clear, blue, beautiful. He owed her an explanation, such as it was. That night had affected her confidence in her command and probably resulted in them being where they were right now.

"And then you came over to me and I thought,

What harm would there be in one drink? I really did intend to tell you. I went to that bar so I'd be alone, and after you arrived, I just didn't feel that way any more. I didn't want to feel alone any more. I didn't mean to deceive you. I really did mean to tell you. A hundred times that night, I meant to tell you."

He paused again, trying to read her face. His arms ached to hold her. His lips burned to kiss her. He felt his body stir with desire. But more than anything he wanted to tell her how much he loved her.

"You never did get around to it, though." Her voice was barely a whisper.

"No."

"And last night? I guess that one was my fault."

"Fault? You think it was a mistake?" He felt a hollowness engulf his soul and he found it difficult to swallow.

"Don't you?" she asked tentatively.

Here was his chance to do the honorable thing and squelch any possibility of something more developing between them. He should tell her that the music and the magic had enchanted them last night. She was his C.O. It shouldn't be repeated. Yet now, so close, he once again couldn't let her go. It would have to end soon enough, he reasoned. Just one more night...

She was watching him intently. The thought of holding her sent tremors of excitement through him. His arousal was immediate.

"No," he said softly, "it wasn't a mistake."

CHAPTER 9

Julie awoke slowly. She was disoriented and highly aroused. The memory of the last few days permeated her consciousness in stages replacing erotic images and sensations, but in both worlds there remained the overriding presence of Matt.

Yesterday he had opened up to her; shown a side of himself that he rarely let others see. They shared a common bond—they were different in an organization that didn't value diversity. She didn't dwell on that, though. It had the potential to shake her whole world, and that made her uncomfortable.

She squirmed. Something was uncomfortable all right—a rock was digging into her side. She rolled slowly onto her back, modestly wrapping the blanket tightly around her naked body, and looked around the cave.

She was mesmerized by the undulating dance of lantern light and shadow along the irregular walls of the cave. She shivered. It was impossible to escape the dampness that radiated from the rocks and ran along the earthen floor.

She could see Matt across the cave. He was sitting, back against a wall, head bent in concentration. He was totally absorbed. Julie squinted to try to see what he was doing. He had a small knife and had found a piece of wood. The delicate, intricate movements of his hands contrasted with the bulk of his broad chest.

It was silent except for the crackling of the fire. Her stomach gave a tremendous growl as she suddenly became aware of a delicious smell filling the cave.

Matt's head shot up and a bright smile lit his face. Her heart swelled.

"Good morning, Major. I'll take that as appreciation for my humble culinary effort." He rose easily and went to the stove.

She sat up, craning her neck to see what he was scooping from the pot. She recognized it as more of Madame Lucie's breakfast mush, but today, it smelled wonderful. Her stomach roared again.

"I'm coming. Patience," Matt teased. He brought a tin plate and spoon to Julie. He also handed her a cup, steaming with hot amber liquid."

"No chocolate?"

"Sorry. I have to save my stash. You never know when you'll encounter a situation where only chocolate will do."

She sniffed the cup and determined it was tea. She then proceeded to eat ravenously, washing it down with the warm liquid.

"Wow, and he cooks, too."

He laughed. "Cooking is one of my more modest accomplishments," he said. "I am much more proficient in other areas."

Julie felt her cheeks go red. She had experienced first-hand some of his talents. Her body stirred with the memory of the previous night.

"What were you doing before I woke up?" she asked to cover her confusion.

"Oh, just a little whittling. I find it helps pass the time." He rose and retrieved the object he had been working on. "Here, I did this for you," he said as he held the piece of wood out to her. "Hummingbirds are incredibly beautiful and delicate, yet also strong and independent," he explained. "Like you." His voice had become husky.

Julie looked down at the bird. Its face reminded her of the festival mask he had selected for her from

Madame Lucie's collection. The vision of making love to him, the wolf, flooded back. At the time she had found the sense of anonymity the masks provided arousing. Had it only been two days ago?

Last night there had been no masks. For the first time they had come together honestly—two people, no more or no less than who they really were. Her body stirred with the memory.

Matt hadn't let go of the bird when she went to take it from him and his hands melded with the textures of the carving. She stroked the hummingbird's extended wings, feeling its feathers morph into gentle fingertips. Its head and neck were smooth, Matt's hands strong and hard.

"Did you know some hummingbirds' wings beat one hundred times per second?" he whispered. "Can you hear?

Julie nodded slowly. She had raised her gaze to his face and was losing herself in his eyes. They were questioning; she wasn't sure she had an answer. In her ears the hummingbird's wings beat one hundred times a second, keeping pace with her own heart. She couldn't breath and closed her eyes as Matt lowered his head.

His lips were soft, yet firm. She felt herself yield to him as he took the bird from her hands and then urged her back onto the ground. She felt as if she were falling through the floor of the cave, spinning through the air toward the center of the earth, out of control. She had only a fraction of a second for her mind to register that giving up control wasn't such a bad thing, before Matt's hot tongue insistently parted her lips and dove deeply into her mouth. She moaned.

While Matt's tongue was exploring her mouth and neck, his hands were working their way down her hips. He pulled her closer to him and she could feel his hardness rising. Her own passion was rising in response and she arched her hips towards him.

"Careful," he cautioned, "this may be habit-forming."

"I don't care," she sobbed, and pulled his mouth back down on hers. Her hands cupped his face, thumbs stroking his cheekbones, still well defined despite a week's growth of beard. Heat surged through her and she felt as if she was on fire. She wanted to feel his skin. She reached up to remove his shirt. He helped her slip it over his head and then began to unwrap the blanket from around her, slowly, deliberately. Matt's gaze never left hers. She wanted him to hurry, but she didn't want it to end. She gasped as the cool, damp air of the cave touched her skin.

His breath was warm on her breasts. "Julie," he moaned as he circled one nipple with his tongue and then took it between his teeth and gently tugged. He cupped her other breast and began rubbing the nipple between his fingers. He had slid his other hand down her back and was urging her hips to meet his own rising passion.

She raked her hands through his hair and down his broad back. Memories of their nights together came racing back—the feel of him, the taste of him, the smell of him. He was right. This was becoming a habit. She couldn't look at him without wanting him.

"Don't stop! Please God, don't stop!" Julie heard herself say over and over.

Matt had shifted position and was slowly making his way down her body, his lips, tongue and hands working in perfect concert to tease her, urge her, drive her wild. It was working. She barely knew where she was anymore. Her entire consciousness was filled with Matt.

Between her legs, his tongue drove deeply into her while his hands kneaded her bottom. Julie's fingers tangled in Matt's hair as though trying to hang on to any sense of reason. But there was no reason. This made no sense at all. Then she was lost. Great spasms cascaded through her body, slowing into tiny shudders, and then silence.

Suddenly he was back, brushing a strand of hair off her face and kissing her again. One hand stroked the back of her neck while the other played with her breasts.

Julie moved her own hands down Matt's back and realized that he had managed to remove his own pants, also. His buttocks were hard and she hungrily pulled him onto her own hips. She was impatient for the feel of him inside her. But first...

She rolled out from underneath Matt and pinned him to the floor, straddling him with her hips. Now, it was her turn to take control. Matt's gaze smoldered. Julie wanted to slowly tease him as he had done with her.

She lowered her head and claimed his mouth, their tongues fought and played. He was making it so difficult for her to make him wait. She couldn't get enough of him.

She could feel his erection pressing against her and he tried to angle his body to gain access to her warm interior.

"Patience," she whispered, a small smile playing on her face.

"There's a difference between patience and torture!"

"Take it up with the Geneva Convention."

But she couldn't find the willpower to make him wait while she tempted and teased him. She grabbed for one of the condoms—they were going through them at a rapid pace, she thought ruefully—and applied it masterfully. Then she raised her body, her gaze locked on Matt's, and slowly lowered herself onto him.

He exhaled gratefully, and their hips began to

work in harmony—slowly, rhythmically at first, then faster and faster as their frenzied union sought completion. Just when she thought she could stand it no more, a giant shudder of release escaped her body, and she felt its echo resonate through Matt.

In the quiet afterward, she lay warmly wrapped in his arms and listened to his ragged breathing.

This is bad, she thought. *This is very, very bad.*

****

Julie and Matt delayed their departure from the cave, and it was well after sunrise before they set out on the path that would lead to the main road. Steam seemed to rise from the earth as the temperature quickly climbed. But at least the rain had stopped—for now.

The rough terrain and narrow trail made progress slow and prevented any conversation. But this time it was a comfortable silence that accompanied their journey.

As Julie stared at Matt's broad back she felt warmth radiating throughout her body and a sigh escaped her.

He turned, questioning.

"Nothing," she said, and smiled.

Matt returned her smile, seeming to know her thoughts. He reached out and tucked a stray bang behind an ear.

Julie felt her knees go weak. Every cell in her body cried out for him to take her in his arms and make love to her as he had done last night and again in the early hours of the morning.

His gaze stared deep into her soul and he brought his lips lightly to hers. He tasted of Madame Lucie's breakfast mush—she was beginning to like it after all—and tea. She responded hungrily, holding his head so he couldn't pull away. The kiss deepened and she felt his tongue glide into her mouth, exploring. The flame that had been keeping her warm despite the wet clothes roared into a fire and she let out a low moan.

She arched against him feeling him harden. Oh God how she wanted him. Here. Now.

What is happening to you, Jules? You know this can't end well.

Reason fought with passion and Julie felt herself being swept up in something she didn't understand. Matt had said he was unable to tell her who he was the night they met despite knowing it was wrong. She fully understood that now. This was wrong—so wrong. And yet she felt powerless to fight it. While she knew she needed to let her troops know she was safe before they launched a full-scale search for her, she was regretting the thought of returning to civilization. Could they possibly hold it off for one more night?

What are you thinking, Jules? Are you really willing to jeopardize your career for a few hours of sex? God, she'd be ridiculed if anyone found out. She was a C.O. She was supposed to set an example!

Through the thick haze of passion she tried to swim back to sanity. She had never before questioned her commitment to her career. But somehow, in Matt's arms, her career seemed very far away, and no longer enough.

Her heartbeat quickened and she caught her breath. Who was Matthew Wolf and how could he affect her so? She should be afraid and yet...

Julie felt Matt still.

"What?" she asked.

"Shhh! Listen."

Julie held her breath and then she heard it—a low rumbling in the distance.

"Bandits?"

"Not unless they've commandeered a tank and a fleet of jeeps."

"Oh God!" Julie sagged as Matt stepped away.

The military.

Julie felt Matt slip something into her hand and push her in front of him, off the path and towards the road. She looked down dumbly. It was a Beretta. His Beretta. She stopped and turned. He shoved her forward.

"Just go, *Major*," he said, emphasizing her title.

Then she understood, and she felt a wave of gratitude sweep through her. Of course, as C.O. she should be the one out front—leading their escape. He had given her his gun so that her troops would think she was the one in control of their situation.

They broke through the forest and stepped out onto the road about twenty yards in front of the convoy. She and Matt held up their hands to forestall any aggression from the forces before they could announce who they were.

Despite their local attire, it was only a few seconds before they were recognized—there weren't too many blonde-haired, blue-eyed, six-foot-tall women on the island.

"Major!" Master Sergeant Murray jumped from the lead vehicle and rushed forward. "Are you all right?"

She drew herself up to her full height and said with much more dignity than she felt, "Yes, Master Sergeant. Thank you. We are both quite all right."

Murray glared at Matt in obvious disapproval. "You should have told us where she was. Who do you think you are?"

She noted Murray's attitude. Matt would have to face a fair bit of scrutiny for his actions. She needed to quell some of their concerns now, before it went too far. She needed to show her confidence in him.

"That's enough, Master Sergeant. This is neither the time nor the place. Lieutenant Wolf has displayed extraordinary tracking and recovery skills in this mission. We can discuss the efficacy of his decisions when we're back at base."

"Yes, ma'am," Murray demurred. He didn't look happy.

"I would like to get back as quickly as possible and change into some dry clothes. I've never been much of a skirt girl," Julie said, trying to break the tension. "We'll take a couple of these jeeps now and the rest of the convoy can return at their leisure."

Julie strode towards one of the two jeeps at the rear of the convoy. With the exception of the driver, the soldiers it carried scrambled out. Then Murray motioned for the driver, also, to vacate the vehicle.

"You two," he said motioning two men dressed in full gear and holding automatic M-16s, "take the Lieutenant."

Julie turned to the second vehicle and was dismayed to see the soldiers *helping* Matt into the jeep with more force than was necessary. She stopped herself from shouting at them. In the scuffle, she saw a paper fall out of his pocket. One of the soldiers picked it up, batting Matt's hand away as he went to grab for it.

She was curious. Matt seemed particularly agitated at the loss of the paper. She stepped out of the jeep and walked towards the soldier.

"Passing notes are we, boys?"

"No, ma'am." The soldier jumped to attention and immediately placed the paper into Julie's outstretched hand.

Matt looked distinctly uncomfortable. She couldn't contain the curse that exploded out of her as she looked down at it. Her knees grew weak and she fought to regain her composure; all eyes were on her.

"Where did you get this?" she said, her voice sounded so strained she barely recognized it as her own. She tried to keep focused on Matt, but her gaze kept falling to the paper she clutched in her hand. It was a drawing of a *vèvè*. The very same *vèvè* she had been meaning to show Matt before she was abducted. But it couldn't be. The bandits had taken it from her. What was Matt doing with this?

As she stared at the ornate grill, its criss-crossed lines accented with stars, she realized this wasn't the drawing she'd made. This one was drawn with a black marker—she had used a blue pen—and these lines were heavier, drawn with more confidence than she'd achieved.

Matt was watching her, a look of grave concern on his face.

"I copied it from the carnival grounds. It is the *lwa* for Ogoun, the mark of the Hougan. Why? Have you seen it before?"

Murray had come to stand beside her and peered at the drawing. "Sweet Jesus!" he whispered.

"Have there been more, Master Sergeant?" Julie asked.

"No, Major. Not since that one."

She turned to Matt. "We found this mark in the courtyard outside the commanders' eating area. It was the reason I came to find you. I wanted you to have it before you headed back out." *Liar!*

Matt turned pale and he tried to get out of the jeep. A soldier held him in. "Is it the same?" he asked. "Are you sure?"

"It's identical," she replied, "right down to the ornamental flourishes on both sides and the pattern on the bottom. Does that mean the Hougan—?"

"I don't know," he said quickly, his expression urging her not to say any more.

"Well, we're not going to solve anything standing in the middle of the road," she said. "I need a hot shower and some of Jimmy's home cooking." She handed the paper back to Matt, their fingers brushed and she held them there just a second longer than necessary.

She turned quickly and took her seat in the jeep.

Murray and two soldiers crawled in after her and fired up the engine. "As quickly as you can, please," she said and the two jeeps roared off down the road.

Julie wondered how long it would take to reach the compound, assuming they didn't crash into another vehicle at this breakneck speed. She felt sorry for the soldiers left behind. The tank—they brought a tank?—and the foot soldiers were probably facing at least two days' travel to get back to Port-au-Paix.

And then it started to rain.

****

Matt sat wedged uncomfortably between two burly soldiers in the back of the jeep, their M-16s lying across their laps, the barrel of one digging uncomfortably into his knee. He surreptitiously snuck an occasional look at the stone-faced man to his left and hoped he was the cautious type—the type that liked to keep the safety on his weapon until he was absolutely sure he was going to have to fire it.

Matt didn't know these men, and they didn't seem inclined to make small talk. He used the silence to go over everything that had happened since they'd arrived in Beljou. If the *vèvè* he had discovered in Liberté was the same as the one at the compound, that would mean they were done by the same person. It seemed likely, too, that that person had made the original *vèvè*—the one to the *lwa* Oya. If the Hougan had drawn the *vèvè* to Ogoun at the carnival, he would have to have drawn the ones in the compound, also. But that didn't make any sense, did it? All this was based on the assumption that Julie was correct and the two *vèvès* to Ogoun were identical. Unless he could see the one from the compound—hopefully someone had the forethought to photograph it—he couldn't know for certain.

Matt's head began to pound as the arguments

went round and round, impossible to resolve without more information. By the time they reached Port-au-Paix some eight hours later—after one brief stop—he was convinced of only one thing: he needed to see Mama Sophie as soon as possible.

It was strangely quiet as they entered the city. Usually the streets were alive with music and dancing, vendors hawking food and baubles to the young people anxious to spend their wages. Lights generally burned all night, as the dance clubs often didn't close their doors until dawn, when their patrons dragged themselves back to their day jobs.

"What's going on?" Matt asked, his voice rough with the first words he had spoken in many hours. "Where is everyone?"

"Curfew," Stone-face said curtly.

Matt turned to the man on his right, hoping he'd be more forthcoming. He was.

"There was a lockdown when the Major didn't return. We had no idea where she was." The soldier glared accusingly at him. "It's not unreasonable to assume someone here was involved, so everyone coming into and out of the city is being checked. Everyone has to observe a sundown curfew."

The jeeps raced down the wide boulevard that led to the Presidential Palace where the troops were headquartered. Matt could see the glow of lights from the compound in the distance.

They paused at the gates to receive the necessary checks and then entered the courtyard. Even for a base that was home to several hundred soldiers, there was a lot of commotion. Something was going on—something beyond the return of an abducted C.O.

They stopped in the middle of the courtyard—Matt's jeep a few yards behind Julie's. She was being rushed by a group of soldiers shouting and gesturing. It didn't look like a welcoming committee.

Matt felt the hair rise on the back of his neck. He was too far back to hear what was being said. Suddenly, Julie jumped from the jeep and raced toward the left wing. Murray was close on her heels as she disappeared through one of the French doors.

"Hey, what's going on?" the driver of Matt's jeep yelled as they all disembarked from the vehicle.

"There's been an injury," someone cried back. "Serious."

Matt approached the group, as interested as the others to find out what was happening. He didn't think he was under arrest, but the two soldiers were apparently under orders to stay close to him. That was going to make his visit to Mama Sophie a bit more challenging, he thought ruefully. Oh well, he never shied away from a challenge.

"What happened?" Stone-face asked.

Matt scanned the crowd for a sign of Wilkes, Brownwell or even Corporal Marshall. He couldn't see any of them.

"An attack. One of the recon guys. Just outside the gate. Not sure of the details. One of the guards spotted him. Brought him in. Half dead."

Matt turned cold. "Who?" He turned to the informant. The man shook his head. Matt grabbed his shirt, thrusting his face very close to the man's. "Who, I said."

"I don't know!" the man cried, trying to get away. Stone-face and one of the other soldiers took hold of Matt's shoulders and pulled him off the man.

"That will be enough, Lieutenant!" said an authoritative voice Matt recognized immediately. The crowd parted as Colonel Sinclair, his face almost as red as his hair, strode towards him. "Let him go, boys."

Matt straightened. Even though he wasn't in uniform, force of habit made him salute the senior officer. "They said it was one of us."

"Yes, I know. Come with me."

Sinclair led Matt toward the left wing of the palace—the medical wing, Matt now remembered.

When they were out of earshot from the crowd Sinclair spoke, not looking at Matt and not slowing his pace. "Captain Wilkes was assaulted earlier this evening. Shot several times, quite seriously. The doctor's trying to stabilize him for transport stateside."

"They said he was outside the compound."

"Yes. He was found just outside the gates as the guard for the evening was changing. I can only assume he startled someone as he was returning to the compound. It was after curfew. No one should have been about."

"So we don't know who did it?"

"Not yet. But the bullets used were military issue—nine millimeter."

"Not one of our men? Surely, Colonel, you can't think..."

"No, no, no. Of course I don't think one of our men attacked Captain Wilkes. I'll be launching an investigation to see if any firearms or ammunition are missing, however. Here we are." Sinclair held open the French door and waved his arm broadly, indicating that Matt should enter. "I will leave you to your unit, Lieutenant. But please *do not* leave the compound. There will be questions, of course. You have a lot to answer for."

Matt walked slowly down the hall. Missing ammunition. Missing firearm. He had a very bad feeling about all of this. He was missing something. It hung in his subconscious just out of reach. "*OH-tuh*!" he cursed in frustration, his fist hitting the wall painfully.

"Doesn't help, sir," Corporal Marshall said, walking towards him. He looked awful. His skin was gray and he staggered a bit, grabbing for support one of the red velvet couches that lined the corridor. “If I thought it would, I’d break every bone in my body.”

“How is he?”

“It’s bad, sir. Really bad.” Marshall had reached him now and managed a feeble salute that Matt returned absently. “He’s lost a lot of blood. They’re not sure he’ll survive the trip back home. I’ve given some of my blood; I’m O-positive, so hopefully that’ll help. Others have donated, too. Major Collins is in there now. It’s good to see you, Lieutenant.”

“Where’s Lieutenant Brownwell?”

“On his way, sir. When Master Sergeant radioed that you’d been found and were on your way in, Colonel Sinclair had me call in both the Captain and the Lieutenant.”

“Yes, I noticed Sinclair is still here.”

“When the Major went missing, he stayed on. Most of his platoon is still here, too. What happened, sir? Where have you and the Major been?”

“Not now.” Matt strode toward Wilkes’ room, stopping on the threshold.

In the glow of a single light, he could see Julie sitting on the edge of the bed holding Wilkes’s hand and speaking to him in a low voice. She was looking intently at Wilkes and Matt could see her eyes, large and luminous, glistening with tears she refused to shed. Matt felt a wave of longing rip through him. Although still dressed in that ridiculous skirt and muddied from their long journey, she was so incredibly beautiful. A golden goddess.

The noise outside had died away, although an occasional shout or dull roar from an engine cut through the air. But even these sounds didn’t interrupt the calmness that Matt felt had now descended on the compound. The C.O. was back, it seemed to say, and everything will be all right.

It was remarkable the impact Julie had been

able make on her troops in the short period of time she'd been their commander. From the looks on the faces of the men in the search party when she stepped out onto the road to the reaction when her jeep pulled into the compound, her troops looked to her for leadership. They needed her. It was a testament to her abilities and her commitment. It was what she had worked so hard to achieve. Finally, it was hers.

Matt watched as her air of serenity encircled the man who was lying in the bed clinging so precariously to life. She was exactly where she needed to be—where she wanted to be.

Blonde-hair, blue-eyes is not for you, Boyo.

Matt felt a pain in his chest so great he wondered if it was possible for a heart to truly break. He should have stuck to the plan he made in Liberté, the night after the carnival when he realized he was in love with her. He should have left her alone—done everything in his power to keep them apart. She was the C.O.; he was her subordinate.

It had been wrong to make love to her in the cave last night—and then again this morning—but he couldn't regret it. While their lovemaking was a sacred memory that he would cherish, they could never have a future together.

The best thing he could do for her now was to back away; to become the subordinate officer he should always have been. He would do everything he could to support her in this mission, and then when it was over they would go their separate ways.

Slowly, he backed out of the room, reluctant to tear his gaze from her—as if this would be the last time he saw her. And it was, he realized. She was his Julie no more.

"Lieutenant Wolf!" The voice of Master Sergeant Murray snapped from behind him. "You're to come with me."

CHAPTER 10

The sun was just peering over the horizon as Julie stepped into her room. Wilkes had stabilized enough that the doctor felt he had a good chance of surviving a flight back home. She had stayed with Wilkes through the night and accompanied him to the helipad. From there he would be airlifted to the airport, put on a plane and transported to medical facilities in Miami. She wanted to stay with him until he was actually on the plane back to America, but there was too much to do here. She had only been gone a little more than a week, yet it felt like a lifetime.

Suzanne was curled up on a chair near Julie's bed, sound asleep.

Bed... sleep, she thought longingly. *Not yet.*

She slowly unbuttoned her blouse. The thought of a shower—of being clean—was more appealing than sleep.

Another pair of hands appeared from behind to remove the blouse.

"*Bonjou*, Madame Major. Welcome home," Suzanne said, her voice hoarse with sleep.

"*Bonjou*, Suzanne. Thank you." She turned to face the girl and was suddenly engulfed in a hug. Suzanne was crying.

"Oh, Madame Major. I was so worried about you. I prayed for you every night. I am so glad you're safe."

Julie held Suzanne, stroking her hair and whispering words of comfort. It seemed that all she had done since she had returned to base was to comfort others: Captain Wilkes, Corporal Marshall who was almost beside himself with grief, Lieutenant Brownwell who had arrived shortly after midnight, and now Suzanne. It was part of being in command, she knew, but it would be so nice to receive some comfort, too. After all, she was the one who'd been kidnapped.

Slowly disentangling herself from Suzanne's embrace, Julie began to remove the rest of her clothing.

"You will sleep now?" Suzanne asked.

"No. I need a shower, and then I must get to my office. I have a lot to do."

"But you must sleep!" Suzanne was insistent.

"Eventually," Julie said, soothingly. "A coffee would be nice. Can you get some coffee sent to my office? I'll be there shortly."

Suzanne nodded. She had begun emptying the pockets of Julie's skirt. Julie had to stifle a laugh. From the way she was handling the skirt, Suzanne must be thinking evil spirits possessed it—she was trying to touch it as little as possible.

She laid the Beretta on the bed beside an assortment of dried fruit, string, pins and other little objects Madame Lucie had felt might be needed for the journey. Suzanne held up the Derringer and gave Julie a quizzical look.

"It's a gun."

Suzanne looked skeptically from Julie to the tiny firearm.

This time Julie didn't hold back her laughter—God, it felt good to laugh. "No, really, it's a gun. Not the most deadly, but it'll do in a pinch."

Suzanne had moved on. The object she now held made Julie's heart beat faster—as fast as the wings of the tiny hummingbird it resembled. Suzanne was turning it over in her hands, her eyes showing her appreciation of the delicate workmanship.

Julie resisted the urge to grab it from the girl. She didn't know why seeing someone else handle it caused her such distress. Maybe it was because the carving represented a secret bond between herself and Matt. Only their two hands had touched it, until now. Like their relationship, she realized with a start.

For the past few days it had just been the two of them. They hadn't had to think about anyone else. But now, like the hummingbird, they couldn't keep others away—couldn't stop others from touching their lives.

Julie stepped into the shower. How was it possible that something as simple as a hot shower could cause such joy? She luxuriated in the warmth of the water as it cascaded down her aching body, and drank in the scent of the shampoo she massaged into her scalp.

She had given herself a lot of time to think on her journey back to the compound. She had rebuffed Murray's attempts to talk about her kidnapping and Matt's actions, telling him she was tired, she needed to process what had happened, and there would be ample time for discussion and a full debriefing when they got back to base. He hadn't been happy, but that was one of the perks of being in command: people had to obey—or at least they were supposed to, Matt being a notable exception.

Matt. Julie's body tingled whenever she thought of him. That had been the biggest problem on the journey back. In the close confines of the jeep, her every move was noted by the Master Sergeant. Every time she'd thought of Matt her body had burned for his touch, and she'd shifted uncomfortably in her seat.

The arrival of the rescue contingent had been so sudden and so unexpected. They hadn't had time to say goodbye or even talk about how they were going to explain all that had happened—the kidnapping, Matt's rescue, why he hadn't immediately called for reinforcements, the Hougan...

When Matt heard the tank and jeeps on the road he had given her his own gun and pushed her forward, making it appear as though she was the one in command of their situation. It had been a generous gesture but, as she now knew, very characteristic of him.

She sighed deeply as she stepped out of the shower and began to towel off. After hours of contemplating their situation, she still didn't know what to do. He loved her. He had told her so over and over last night. And while that should cause her and her career great concern, instead she felt elated. That could only mean one thing. And if she had any doubts about it before, her reaction to Suzanne's handling of the hummingbird confirmed it for her. Julie loved him, too.

It was much more than just a physical attraction. It was so much more than just great sex. Julie wanted a relationship; and although there hadn't been time to talk about it, she was pretty sure Matt felt the same way. He had to. They connected on so many levels. He had told her things about his past—painful things—that he hadn't told anyone else. A man didn't do that for a fling, or a roll in the sack.

But what to do? She was his commanding officer, and the military had rules—very strict rules—about fraternization.

There had to be a way to work this out. The military couldn't stop people from falling in love; it couldn't keep people apart just because of rank. This couldn't be the first time a senior officer had fallen in love with a junior officer—maybe even with an enlisted soldier.

But what if there isn't a way, Jules. Would you...?

No. She wouldn't think about that now. There

had to be a way.

She desperately wanted to see Matt, to talk to him, to...

But first, she needed to do a bit of research into their situation. And even before that, she needed to get to her office and see what had been happening in Beljou during her absence.

****

Julie's heart plunged as she recognized the familiar silhouette of the man in her office. She barely had time to mask her shock before he turned to her. He took several steps towards her, a strange, unfamiliar look on his face. Then suddenly his features hardened and he stopped.

"You look well," the General said.

"I didn't know you were here, General." She saluted automatically.

"I asked that you not be told last night. You had quite enough to deal with." He waved his arm, indicating that she should sit. "That cook—Jimmy—brought some coffee. Shall I pour?"

He was making her feel like she was a guest in her own office, dammit! *Keep your cool, Jules.* She nodded, not trusting herself to speak. But defiantly, she remained standing.

"What brings you here?" She took the cup, gripping it tightly to help steady her nerves. The aroma was heaven.

Coffee in hand, the General went to sit behind Julie's desk and then paused as if thinking better of it, and selected one of the overly-ornate cushioned chairs that she used for guests.

"Why do you *think* I came? You were kidnapped by God-knows-who and no one seemed to have any answers."

"I hardly think the kidnapping of a lowly Major warrants a visit from the Army Chief of Staff."

"It's always the same with you," the General said

in exasperation. "You are my daughter. Of course I'm going to come. You are the only one who thinks it's unusual for me to be here. Even the Secretary of Defense thinks I should be here."

"You took this to the Secretary of Defense?" Julie was mortified.

"Of course the Secretary was involved. So was the President. It's a very serious matter when the head of a military operation is kidnapped. We needed to ensure the support of the Beljouan President and his resources. That's not something Master Sergeant Murray, or even Colonel Sinclair, can do."

Julie sat stunned, for the first time the full implication of her kidnapping becoming apparent. Matt had been right. Her abduction had the potential to set off a powder keg on the island, the repercussions of which could seriously hurt the people of Beljou.

"What happens now?"

"We're still trying to get to the bottom of this. Lieutenant Wolf is not being very helpful. I think he knows more about who took you than he's saying."

"How is he?" The words were out of Julie's mouth before she could stop them.

The General eyed her carefully before answering. "It doesn't look good for him. I can't tell you the number of regs he's broken, and yet he remains uncooperative."

"But he rescued me."

"His cowboy actions were irresponsible! If he knew or even suspected where you were, he should have reported it. We could have gotten you out of there much faster. And maybe we would have been able to catch the men who did this. No, Lieutenant Wolf has a lot to answer for."

"He did what he thought was right."

"It's not his job to think!" The General jumped up

suddenly, his deep voice filling the expansive office, "It's his job to follow orders."

This was an argument Julie knew she wasn't going to win. She didn't even disagree with the General's attitude—in theory. But this wasn't theory. This was Matt. Nevertheless she let it drop. "Well, we can discuss this further after I've submitted my report." She stalked over to her desk and sank into the chair, her legs unable to hold her any longer.

"Fine," said the General, his tone softening. "You catch up, and we'll talk again later."

Julie stared for several long moments at the door the General had closed when he left the room. Damn him anyway! He could still make her feel as childish as he had when he caught her sneaking out of the house to meet her boyfriend when she was sixteen.

Julie jumped at the knock on her door. *Now what?* "Come."

She was unprepared to see Matt enter the room. He closed the door, but didn't come further into the office.

Her heart jumped at the sight of him, and she felt a warm flush race over her body. He looked wonderfully handsome, dressed in his full uniform. And he had shaved. Julie's fingers ached to stroke the smooth, strong jaw. She rounded her desk towards him, and was stopped by the unreceptive look in his eyes.

"Major Collins," he said, stepping to attention and saluting her.

"Lieutenant?" She laughed, returning the salute. What was he playing at? After all this time was he finally going to fall in line and behave as a model soldier? Had she been able to effect that kind of change on him? She doubted it. Any second he would break character and sweep her into his arms. She could hardly wait.

"Permission to speak freely, ma'am."

"Granted." Any moment now...

"I'm here on behalf of my unit. We have suffered a terrible loss with the injury to Captain Wilkes. I'm here to let you know that as the next senior officer, I am prepared to assume Captain Wilkes's responsibility and take command of the unit."

She stared at him, stunned. Was he serious? "You want to be given command of recon?" she was eventually able to ask.

"Yes, ma'am. I am the senior officer in our unit."

Her mind was racing. This was totally unexpected. But was it out of character for him? Hadn't he complained that he was passed over—that he felt he *deserved* to be in command of his unit? "Do you know what you're asking?" she said slowly.

"Yes, ma'am." For the first time Matt's air of confidence seemed to waver.

"No, Lieutenant, I don't think you do." Julie raised her gaze to Matt's, pleading with him to understand. How could he ask this of her? Now? Surely he had to understand that there were rules, regulations, protocols that needed to be followed. "I've just met with the Army Chief of Staff. He and the senior command have a lot of concern about your actions, and your lack of cooperation in the investigation into my kidnapping."

"I know that." His voice was quiet. "You know the truth, though. You understand why I did what I did."

"I do. I even agree with you. But you're asking me to promote you when I'm not even sure I can stop them from court-martialing you." It was killing her to take his dream away from him, but she had to make him understand how precarious his situation was. "Besides, given your reputation, I would have difficulty promoting you even in the best of circumstances."

Julie's heart clenched as she saw the hurt in his eyes. She moved closer, wanting to comfort him—ease his pain.

He stepped backwards, his back now pressed tightly against the door. "That reputation is based on rumor and innuendo," he said stiffly. "There is no factual basis for it."

"But it's a perception of you and your tactics that you've allowed to persist—even cultivated at times."

"It's the type of work I do," his voice strained. "It's served the Army well."

Julie knew it was true, and terribly unfair. He was the best at what he did, and a large part of that was due to how he did it. "It's also what's held you back."

"I thought you, of all people, would understand," he said.

"I do understand," she said. "But what do you expect me to do about it? It's a façade you've created for yourself. Would it have hurt for you to let your senior officer know that you're really not the Lothario everyone thinks you are? That it's an act?"

"But I did let my senior officer know. I let you know. You're the C.O. And I thought with your background..."

Warning bells were going off in Julie's head and she felt her knees weaken. She was having trouble focusing on what Matt was saying. Her worst fear was pushing all rational thought out of her head. "I don't understand," she said weakly, and grabbed the back of one of the ornate chairs for support. "Do you mean my family?"

"No!"

"It's my father, you mean!" She felt anger spark through her. She pulled herself up to her full height and glared at Matt. "You think that because my father is the Army Chief of Staff I can just ignore all the stuff on your record and promote you." She was building a scenario in her head—a familiar scenario of deception, and her mind was automatically returning to the old scripts. She should have known that it wasn't her he was really interested in. He wanted what the General's daughter could do for him—just like all the others.

"Julie, please..." he began but was interrupted.

"It's not me you want, it's my father! Well it's not going to work. I'm the C.O. here. I make the decisions." She could feel her anger starting to dissipate. She could not show any weakness now. He had hurt her. She struck back. "I wonder if you really believe all that crap about not trusting the military to respond appropriately to my kidnapping. Maybe you just wanted more time to work on me. Well you can forget about any promotion. I see your true colors, now. Dismissed!"

"Julie..."

"Get out. Now!"

Matt nodded, turned and left without another word.

"No," Julie whispered, giving in to her anguish. How could she have been so stupid? How could she have allowed herself to believe that Matt was different from all the other people in her life who had only wanted her for what she represented, what they thought she could do for them? He had deceived her from the start.

Stupid! Stupid! Stupid! Julie's body convulsed with great sobs of despair. She had had her heart broken before—by boys who claimed to love her, by friends who claimed to like her, by co-workers who claimed to respect her—but it had never hurt like this.

Julie wasn't sure she could go on. She wasn't even sure she wanted to. Her future loomed before her, vast and empty.

Only a few moments ago, despite her father's

unwelcome appearance, she had felt on top of the world. She had everything—her own command, and a man who loved her. There was no obstacle she couldn't overcome.

You still have your command, Jules.

But it was no longer enough.

****

Matt walked the perimeter of the compound several times trying to cool his anger. He wasn't mad at Julie. He was mad at himself. How could he have put her in that position? Of course she couldn't promote him. Even knowing the truth, it would be a career-ending move for her. Especially now.

The look she gave him when he entered her office almost undid him. Her joy at seeing him showed dazzlingly on her face. It had taken superhuman restraint not to rush to take her in his arms. He had kept as much physical distance between them as possible in the last twenty-four hours. He had to.

And now, thanks to his actions, he had also succeeded in putting an emotional distance between them. That hadn't been his intention. He hadn't wanted to hurt her. And he certainly hadn't wanted to add to her insecurities about her own self-worth. That was the worst of it.

Any feelings Julie had for him were now gone. It was for the best, he kept telling himself. Still, it hurt to know how much he would give up for her, and how easily she could assume the worst of him. After all they had shared, how could she think he had been using her? He would do anything for her. He would take a bullet for her to keep her dreams safe. He would walk away from her. This was like dying to him.

Enough! Thinking about Julie and her reaction wasn't getting him anywhere. There were still questions about the kidnapping that needed answers. If both he and Julie were going to get out of this mess with their reputations relatively unscathed he had to pull himself out of his self-pity and find the Hougan. He knew just where to start—with Mama Sophie.

The sun was high in the sky, although there were dark clouds in the distance threatening rain. With a vehicle he figured he could make it to the village and back before the storm hit.

In the garage, the burly mechanic pointed to a jeep. He seemed reluctant to allow Matt to take it, so Matt pulled rank. Since the man hadn't been told specifically to refuse Matt transportation, he had to let it go.

The gate, however, was a different matter.

"No, sir." Although he shifted uncomfortably from foot to foot and refused to meet Matt's gaze, the young private stood his ground. "I've got orders. You're confined to base."

Frustrated, Matt returned the jeep to the motor pool, ignoring the smirk of the burly mechanic.

Now what? He had to get to Mama Sophie. He could make himself up as a local and slip away with the exiting day shift. It had worked before. No, that would certainly get him court-martialed. And if Julie was trying to save his skin, it would call her judgment even further into question.

He was truly stuck between the proverbial rock and a hard place. If he told the General and Colonel Sinclair his suspicions, they would send the military in, guns a-blazing, and all the work he had done to keep the situation under control would be lost. Alone, he could take the Hougan down. He had to bring him to justice in a way that wouldn't make the man a martyr, a way that wouldn't give the Hougan the power he so desperately sought. He just had to find him. Mama Sophie was the key; he knew it in his gut. But because they didn't know the whole story, the General and Colonel Sinclair were keeping him from getting to her.

"Lieutenant Wolf! Lieutenant Wolf!"

Despite his aggravation with his current situation, Matt couldn't help but smile as he recognized young James racing towards him from across the courtyard, accompanied by the mangy dog. Both the boy and the dog looked much better-nourished than the last time he had seen them.

The boy skidded to a stop and the dog began sniffing Matt's pocket. "Hello, James. How have you been? I see you've been allowed to keep our friend, here." Matt reached down to scratch the dog's head.

"Well, I'm not really supposed to allow him to run around the compound. Mama would be very angry with me if she found out. But he needs exercise, no? And the soldiers don't seem to mind...very much. Do you have candy?"

"I think I might have a piece or two in here somewhere," Matt said reaching into his pocket and withdrawing a brand new, wrapped chocolate bar he had picked up earlier that morning. He laughed as he saw James' eyes widen. Not just candy, but chocolate!

"So you are getting along well, then?" Matt asked as he and James sat down on a bench in the garden. He teased James by opening the candy bar with deliberate slowness.

"Oh, yes. We are doing quite well," he replied without turning his gaze away from Matt's hands. "Mama seems happy. She is working in the laundry. I miss my friends sometimes, and *Grandmère*, too."

"You haven't seen her since you've been here?"

"No, and Mama refuses me to talk about her."

The candy bar now open and shared, the two sat in comfortable silence, mouths full of creamy milk chocolate. The dog seemed to have settled in for the long term, lying across Matt's feet.

Matt's mind returned to the delicate problem of

speaking with Mama Sophie. Perhaps he could use James to get a message to her; to have her come to see him at the compound. But almost as soon as the thought came to mind, he dismissed it as too dangerous for the boy. Who knew what would happen to James if he returned to his village. Matt didn't think he was in danger from Mama Sophie, but there were others—especially now.

"James! Where are you?" An angry voice pierced Matt's musings, and he felt James stiffen in apprehension.

"I'm here, Mama," he called. "With Lieutenant Wolf."

Matt smiled. The boy was hoping his presence would save him from his mother's wrath. He stood and turned to see the brave woman from the village hurrying towards them. If James hadn't identified her as his mother, Matt would never have guessed this was the same woman he had encountered a week ago. Her color had improved, and as she stood before him, she had a regal bearing.

"It is very nice to see you again," Matt said. "Don't be angry with James. He and I were just catching up."

The woman smiled feebly. "Thank you, Lieutenant. You and your people have been very good to James and me—even allowing James to keep his pet."

"Would you like to join us? We were just sharing some chocolate."

Although she looked as if she would refuse, the lure of chocolate was too great, and she nodded.

"Good. I'm afraid I don't know your name. We didn't have much time for conversation when we last met." She was worried about something, Matt could see it in her eyes. Hopefully, it was some small domestic matter, but his senses told him that it was something more. He needed to gain her confidence in order to find out what was going on.

"Marie. I'm called Marie," she said, taking a piece of chocolate.

"It's nice to meet you, Marie. I understand you're working in the laundry."

Marie gave her son a sharp, unhappy look. James flushed and slid off the bench to roll on the ground with his dog.

"Yes," she said.

"Is there a problem with the laundry?" Matt asked. "I remember you didn't want to work in the kitchens..."

"No," she said quickly. "There is no problem with the laundry. I am quite satisfied there."

"I am curious about the kitchen, though. The laundry must be very hot and difficult, especially with all the rain. "Surely, the kitchen would be better."

"No!" Marie turned to Matt, a look of panic on her face. "I cannot go to the kitchen. I'm not sure I should even be outside of the laundry now, in the daylight." She jumped up quickly. "James! Come. We must go. Goodbye, Lieutenant."

"Wait!" Matt rose quickly, desperate to stop her from leaving. "I didn't mean to upset you. I'd like to help."

"You have done too much for us already. Please, James. We must return to our rooms."

"But Mama," James whined, "the rain has stopped and we have only just come out. Please, can we not stay a bit longer?"

"No. We've taken too much of a risk already."

"Risk?" Matt was confused. "What kind of risk is there here? Surely you know you're safe? Nothing will happen to you here."

"Oh, monsieur, I wish that was the case. You have been so kind..."

With horror Matt realized the woman was

crying. James had come to his mother and was now embracing her, murmuring words of comfort.

"I'm sorry, I just don't understand," Matt said.

James looked up at him, arms still around his mother's waist. "It has been wonderful these last few days. We have had so much freedom—been able to wander around the compound without fear. But *he* has come back and so now we must hide ourselves—keep to the laundry and the women's rooms."

"Who is back? Who are you afraid of?"

"*Grandpère.*"

Matt stepped back as if he had been struck. That wasn't possible. Madame Lucie had confirmed Matt's suspicion that Mama Sophie's husband—James' grandfather—and the Hougan were one and the same. But he could have only just returned to the capital. And ensconced in the safety of the compound, how could they know?

"How do you know he's back?"

"I saw him."

"You saw him?" he asked dubiously. "Where?"

There had to be some mistake. Perhaps the boy had had a nightmare about his grandfather coming to get him. But that didn't explain Marie's fear.

"Here."

"Here? In the compound?" Matt realized both Marie and James were looking at him as if he had lost his faculties. He was scrambling to latch on to something that was just out of reach. *Slow down; take it a step at a time.*

It was unbelievable that the Hougan would come to the compound and allow himself to be seen. And yet, both James and his mother were absolutely convinced that he had.

His boldness wasn't in doubt. This wasn't the first time he had come to the compound. He'd been here the day they arrived and had daringly drawn the *vèvè* to Oya outside of Julie's office. And then, again, to leave the *vèvè* to Ogoun.

And then there was Wilkes. He was almost killed by someone with a nine-millimeter gun using military-issue ammunition. Was he attacked by someone trying to get into the compound? That would mean it was someone who had recently arrived in Port-au-Paix.

If James and Marie were correct, the Hougan *had* gotten into the compound—and he had been able to do so at a time when security had been significantly tightened.

And there was something else. Something that had been bothering him from the first time he had seen the Hougan, something familiar about the man; the way he moved.

Slowly, it was all coming together. Piece by piece he was solving the puzzle. And then, suddenly, it made sense.

Of course he was here. He had been here all along. Who else had full access to the entire compound, and was privy to the routines and schedules of the senior officers? Who else could come and go without question? Who else held a firm, divine-like hold on the people working under him? Who else would cause Marie to fear being assigned to the kitchens?

Only one man. And Matt knew who he was.

CHAPTER 11

Julie felt the bench sag as someone sat down beside her. Desperate to be alone, she turned to order them away and found herself looking at the General. His posture was rigid and his eyes stared straight ahead.

"I've had a long day, General. I really don't want to argue with you right now," she snapped.

"Good. Then perhaps you'll listen to what I have to say for a change."

Julie sighed. The fight had gone out of her. When she had finally been able to get up off the floor after Matt left, she spent the better part of the day trying to concentrate on the reports that had piled up in her absence. It didn't work. She couldn't focus on anything other than her own misery. Finally, she had given up and come to her favorite spot in the palace's vast gardens.

"I just want to be by myself right now. Can't you leave me alone?"

"Do you know the name of the tree you're sitting under?" the General asked, ignoring Julie's plea. "It's called the *sabliye* tree—the forgetting tree. According to legend, African slaves were made to walk under the *sabliye* tree before they were packed onto ships and brought to work on the plantations of Beljou and the other islands in the Caribbean Sea."

"Did it work? Did they forget?"

"Does it look like it did? This area is full of the customs and traditions from not just the Africans, but all the people who came here. You can leave your home, your friends, your family. You can travel to the other side of the world. But you can't forget who you are, no matter how hard you try. It follows you everywhere you go."

"Tell me something I don't know," Julie said bitterly.

"Okay, how's this? You are trying so hard to run away from *what* you are that you are allowing it to define *who* you are."

"You don't understand what it's like to be me—to be the daughter of the Army Chief of Staff, the sister of two of the youngest colonels in the military. And most people don't even know about Granddad. No one sees me for me. Everything is about the family name, the family honor. Nobody really wants to be with me, they're just looking for a way to get close to you. Why can't I be loved for me?"

The General wrapped his arms around Julie and pulled her close. She didn't resist. He kissed her brow and allowed her to sob into his chest. After a few minutes, she sat back and wiped her eyes on her sleeve.

"You know the last time you cried in my arms?" he asked very softly.

Julie shook her head, unable to speak.

"You were, maybe, four. I was leaving on a mission—I can't remember where—and wouldn't see you for a very long time. You were begging me to stay. When I returned, you had changed, grown up, matured—well, mature for a five-year-old. But something had happened to make you wise to the ways of the world. Something, or more likely someone, had stolen your innocence."

"Mrs. Clarke, my kindergarten teacher. She gave me a gold star on my coloring when I knew I didn't deserve it. I was always terrible at art. She said to be sure to tell my father how much she liked my drawings."

"It broke my heart when I got home. I didn't

know how to fix things for you. Maybe we should have moved off the base so you could be away from it. But I couldn't do that to your mother. She relied on the other wives for support, especially when I was away. She's fine, by the way. Your mother. Took the news of your disappearance much better than I did. I called her when we heard you were safe. She sends her love."

Julie felt a stab of guilt. The reprimand was well deserved. She had been so annoyed to see the General she hadn't thought about what effect the whole situation would have on her mother. "I'll call her later."

"Anyway," the General continued, "I waited and hoped things would improve. But unfortunately, Mrs. Clarke was just the first in a long line of users. Am I right?"

"I just want people to see *me*!"

"I know. It is so much easier for your brothers. They're happy to distinguish the family name—to be part of the Collins legacy. But that's not who you are. That's why I fought you so hard when you said you wanted to join the military. I worried about whether you could ever be happy in this life. And even more than that, I worried that we would never be able to have a close personal relationship, when everyday you'd be fighting the demon of the Collins name."

"Why are you telling me this now?"

"I should think that was obvious. When Murray called me to say you'd been abducted, I felt as if my world had collapsed. What if I lost you without ever telling you how much I love you?"

"So Murray *is* your man?"

The General snorted. "Typical Julie: cut to the chase. I open up myself to you after all these years, I tell you how I feel, and you want to quiz me about one of my men."

"I'm just trying to understand everything."

"Yes, Murray is 'one of mine.' He's been with me for years. I have complete confidence in him. That's why I assigned him to you."

"But he was still working for you? Reporting on me?"

"Reporting on you would not be completely accurate. I assigned him to you because he's an excellent soldier and would be an asset on any mission. In addition, I asked him to look out for you. It's difficult enough for a woman C.O. in the field, but even more so if that woman is *my* daughter. My instruction to Murray was to quell any gossip or rumors before they got out of hand. I wanted to make sure you received the respect your rank deserved. And, occasionally, I'd call and ask him how it was going for you."

"You were trying to make it easier for me? To help me succeed?" Julie had all but convinced herself that it was impossible for him to interfere in her career. Had she been wrong about this, too?

"Not overtly, and certainly not in any way that gave you preferential treatment," the General said quickly. "I was very clear with Murray. You were to be allowed to succeed or fail on your own merit. His job was just to make sure it was allowed to happen naturally."

"I don't believe it," Julie said slowly, the implications of the General's remarks sinking in. She turned to her father, her eyes bright with fresh tears. "Are you saying you actually support my military career?"

"Of course. You're one hell of a soldier. We could use more like you. I had Murray's word that everything was going well, but when I got here and saw how committed your troops were to you, I was very impressed. And very proud."

"Proud?" Julie was afraid to believe what she

was hearing. "You're proud of me?"

"Of course!"

"But I was kidnapped!"

"So? You survived. That's all that matters. That's no more, or no less, than I'd hope for from any of my men."

"Oh, Daddy!" Julie fell into her father's arms. "I was so scared." She was thirty-eight years old and here she was, cuddling up next to her father. It felt wonderful. Did a girl ever stop needing her father? She didn't know. All she knew was that she finally *believed* that she had his love and acceptance, and it made all the difference in the world.

A little while later, still resting against her father's chest, she said, "I still don't know how to deal with the people who just want me for my family name."

"I would think that by now you'd see them coming from a mile away."

"I thought so, too." She wanted desperately to open up to him, but a part of her was still fearful of disappointing him. She felt his embrace tighten slightly as though urging her to trust him. She took a deep breath, her decision made. "I met someone. I didn't mean for it to happen. I'm in love with him." Julie paused to compose herself. "I thought he loved me, too, but I was wrong."

"Is it someone here?"

Julie nodded.

"Are you so sure you're wrong?"

"It's Lieutenant Wolf. Please, please don't hold it against him. I know his rescue of me was unorthodox, but he had his reasons. He was trying to save the mission, trying to protect the people of Beljou who have already been through so much. I think he was right to do what he did."

"I hope sometime one or the other of you will give me a full briefing on this, but for now, my concern is you. Tell me, why do you think he was using you?"

The General sat quietly while Julie recounted the conversation she and Matt had earlier in the day. "My background! Can you believe it? I was so certain he didn't care about any of that. How could I be so stupid?"

"Hush, Jules. I know it sounds bad, but are you sure? I've had several opportunities to speak with Lieutenant Wolf and despite the current situation he strikes me as a man with integrity. I've read his record and know that his mission-success rate is countered by a somewhat dubious reputation with the ladies, but that reputation and what you're talking about don't jibe with the man I've been dealing with."

"He said—"

"I heard you. But that could have meant anything. Let me ask you this: if that man can be so caring about the people of Beljou—willing to risk his career for their well-being—what do you think he would do for someone he loved?"

****

The palace kitchen was in a separate building, located just behind the wing that housed the grand dining hall, which was now being used as the general mess. It had been the custom a hundred and fifty years ago, when the palace had been built, to keep the kitchen away from the main building in order to reduce the risk of fire. Although all the modern conveniences of the developed world had come to the capital—electricity, running water, and indoor flush toilets—the kitchen had remained detached.

Matt approached cautiously and peered in the window, impressed by what he saw. The running of the kitchen was like the running of a small army. The men and boys who worked there—there were no women—were divided into units: those who went to market, those who cleaned vegetables, those who prepared the meats, those who cooked the *viv*, those who ushered the great trolleys of food to the main building and back again, those who served the meals, and those who cleaned up afterwards. And overseeing it all was Jimmy.

Matt checked his Beretta. Corporal Marshall had returned it to him after the interrogation by the General and Colonel Sinclair. They may have confined him to base, but at least they'd given him his firearm back. That was a positive sign—maybe.

He needed to get Jimmy alone. Matt couldn't be sure how many of the kitchen workers were in league with the Hougan. While he didn't want to take him in the open, it would be dangerous to allow him to reach the palace proper.

On his last visit, Matt had discovered the elaborate network of secret corridors that ran throughout the palace. Their purpose was to conceal the help from the royal family and its guests. They would also provide the perfect escape route for Jimmy.

He could be patient when he had to be. He couldn't leave the base anyway, so he might as well bide his time until an opportunity presented itself.

He didn't have to wait long. While Jimmy relished his role as head of the kitchen, he didn't much like staying in the hot building and spent a lot of his time outside, smoking. Matt quietly followed Jimmy as he walked to a secluded garden between the kitchen and the palace. He watched him sit down on a bench, withdraw a package of tobacco and some rolling papers, roll a cigarette, and lean back comfortably to enjoy his vice.

"You know smoking will kill you," Matt said amicably, approaching the startled Jimmy. He had his Beretta tucked into his waistband behind his back.

"Lieutenant, I am surprised to see you."

"Really? You knew we were back, Major Collins and me."

"Yes. I was very glad to hear you had been rescued."

"Rescued? Oh, no. We were just on our way back from the carnival at Liberté and we came across some of our boys. They offered us a ride home, so we accepted."

"But I thought Major Collins had been kidnapped by... by rebels." Jimmy was looking very uncomfortable.

Matt smiled. He planned to confuse Jimmy. He just had to be careful the man didn't bolt before he got what he wanted from him. "What would make you think that Major Collins was kidnapped? And by rebels? There aren't any rebels. They've all been put down by the very efficient action of Colonel Sinclair and the Three-Eighty-Six."

"Yes, of course you are right, Lieutenant. I'm just a poor villager who works in the kitchen. I don't understand politics or armies."

"Oh, come now, Jimmy. We both know that's not true. You can be a very powerful and persuasive speaker when you want to be. Your speech to the crowd in Liberté on the weekend sent shivers down my spine."

"I really don't know what you're talking about. I was at home on the weekend, with my family. You can ask them. I've never even been to Liberté." Jimmy had gotten to his feet and his eyes were darting left and right, looking for an escape.

"Oh, I'm sure your family will vouch for you. But you see, I happen to know that not only were you in Liberté this weekend, you were born there, and lived there up until the time you killed your family and convinced one of the mambos to run away with you."

"I'm sorry, Lieutenant, you must have me

confused with someone else." Jimmy's tone had changed from one of fear and submission to the more cultured, powerful tenor of the Hougan. He no longer stooped, his loose limbs now tightened into a stiff, dignified pose and he looked directly into Matt's eyes.

"That's better," Matt said. "Let's not play games. Jimmy, Hougan, P'tee Jay—call yourself whatever you wish—you have a lot to answer for."

"You are mistaken if you think you can bring me down."

"And you're mistaken, if you think I can't."

The Hougan turned suddenly and darted towards an opening in the shrubs surrounding the garden. He stopped as the bullet whizzed past his head and struck a marble statue, sending shards of rock into the air.

"No more warnings," Matt said ominously. "Sit."

Slowly, the Hougan returned to the bench.

"No, as much as I think you deserve it, I'm not going to kill you in cold blood," Matt said, noting the man's wary look at the Beretta. "But make a move and I won't hesitate to shoot you."

"All right, Lieutenant, take me in. Put me on trial. Convict me, even. The people will rise in protest. Blood will run through the streets. My cause will not be lost."

"And what cause is that?"

"We have lost our way. The *lwas* are angry with us for forgetting them. Their betrayal must be avenged. Our people must come back to the faith that ties us with our land."

"Give me a break," Matt said dismissively. "This isn't a spiritual battle. It isn't even a political one. It's about power and greed. If you can destabilize the country, you and your bandit friends can extort money and basically do whatever you want."

"I would have thought that after what the

Americans did to *your people* you would be more sympathetic to our cause."

Matt refused to rise to the bait. "That's the problem. Your 'cause' is *you.* I have more sympathy for the rebels we've just put down than I do for you and your kind. At least they were fighting for something—another vision of what Beljou should be, misguided as it was."

"Why have you not arrested me yet? I am prepared to legally defend myself."

"I'm getting around to arresting you. But first, I want something from you."

"Hah! I will give you nothing."

"I want the gun, the one you took from Major Collins and used to attack Captain Wilkes."

"I don't have any gun. If I did I would use it to shoot you now."

"After the attack on Wilkes, I wouldn't expect you to have it on you. But I certainly hope you remember where you put it. Without that gun I'm not prepared to be lenient."

"Lenient? How?"

"Well, first of all, your dreams of a big public trial aren't going to come true. As you are currently an employee of the American military, you'll be sent to America and tried in a military court. We don't allow Court-TV to broadcast our trials, so you'll have no sympathetic audience. And you'll find the jury—all military officers—is unlikely to be compassionate when a C.O., the *daughter of the Army Chief of Staff* no less, has been kidnapped. And if you add the near-killing of Captain Wilkes... Well, let's just say you don't have enough years left in your pitiful life to serve your full sentence."

"And if I give you the gun?"

Matt noted an edge of panic had slipped into the Hougan's voice. When it came right down to it, all bullies were cowards underneath. "Then I'd be prepared to accept a confession. Make no mistake: you will go to jail. It's just a matter of whether or not you'll outlive your sentence."

Recognizing defeat, the Hougan hunched forward and placed his head in his hands. "Okay," he said, his voice barely a whisper. "I hid the gun in a cabinet in one of the passageways we use."

"Up." Matt tapped him lightly with the barrel of his gun. "Let's get the gun, and then you can go confess to the General."

"I had no idea she was *his* daughter," the prisoner whimpered.

"Yeah, that was pretty rotten luck."

Matt allowed the Hougan to lead him into the corridor that ran along the inside of the dining wing. He was fairly certain the man had been broken, but he wasn't willing to let down his guard, even slightly, and kept the Beretta pressed close to the Hougan's ribs. Although they encountered several of the servers, who stared at them in surprise, they were allowed to pass without comment.

The Hougan stopped suddenly, wincing as the gun barrel dug into his back. He began to open a cabinet when Matt stopped him.

"I'll do it."

Edging his prisoner aside, Matt opened the cabinet.

"Inside the serving bowl at the back."

Matt nodded. With his free hand, he reached into the cabinet and felt for the lid of the big serving bowl. He removed it, careful not to let its fall damage other dishes on the shelf. There it was. He could feel the cold metal as he withdrew the firearm. The Browning nine-millimeter. Julie's gun.

"Where does this go?" Matt asked motioning towards the nearest door.

"It is Master Sergeant Murray's office."

"Perfect. After you."

Matt could have laughed out loud at the look of surprise on Murray's face as a panel on the wall slid open. Matt followed Jimmy through it into Murray's office.

"Master Sergeant Murray." Matt smiled brilliantly. "I believe Jimmy has something he wants to tell you. I'd love to stay, but I really must return this gun to Major Collins. I don't think we're going to need it, given Jimmy's cooperation. However, if you do, I imagine the Major would be happy to let you borrow it."

Without another word, Matt walked out of the office.

He was feeling pretty good about himself. He had saved the girl. And now he had caught the bad guy. Not bad for a few days' work. There was only one thing left to do. After everything else, it should be easy, but it was the thing that terrified him most. And yet, in his heart, he knew it was the only thing he could do—the last piece that would safeguard Julie's reputation. He would do it for her.

Matt squared his shoulders. After one quick stop to drop the gun off in Julie's office, he was headed to the room that had been temporarily assigned as the General's office.

****

Someone he loved. Those were the words her dad had used. *Was it possible she had been wrong about Matt?*

Julie walked slowly down the hall towards her sleeping quarters. She had left her father at his office after begging off dinner saying she didn't want to appear in front of the troops with swollen, red eyes; not a good image for a C.O. In truth, she needed time to process all that had happened. Seeming to understand her need to be alone, the General let her go with a commitment for breakfast the next morning.

She sat down heavily on her bed. A bone-aching tiredness wracked her body and her head screamed for peace. At this moment there was nothing she wanted more than to sleep, to escape into oblivion for a few hours.

She hadn't slept in two days—not since the night in the cave when she had lain in Matt's arms. And there hadn't been much sleep that night. A jolt of grief knotted her gut, and she grabbed her pillow and hugged it close.

Could her father be right about Matt? Could she have misunderstood?

No, he had been so cold and distant when he came to see her earlier. Her father had only spent a few hours with him. She had spent days. She knew him better than anyone. Or at least she'd thought she did.

What would he do for someone he loved? Julie tried to block that question from her mind. She felt incapable of dealing with it now. She was tired, her emotions were raw. Yet, again and again, her father's words kept coming back. They wouldn't be dismissed.

Okay, Jules, what would he do for someone he loved?

When she finally allowed the question some space in her mind, the answer came to her immediately. It thundered into her consciousness, taking her breath away.

Anything. Everything.

If Matt loved her, why had he been so distant towards her? He'd barely looked at her. He had stayed as far away from her as was humanly possible in the office. It was as if he was afraid of her.

Afraid of her? Or afraid of hurting her?

Yet he had hurt her. It was a hurt so deep she wasn't sure she would ever recover.

It was so unlike him, though. Her father was right. Matt was a man of integrity. He was a man who had shown tremendous respect for the people of this island. He had jeopardized his career for them.

Julie had confided her hopes and fears to him. He knew how important her career was to her. That was obvious when he had fallen back before meeting the rescue convoy. He had given her his own gun. From the moment her men had spotted them, he had behaved as the perfect subordinate to her.

She was his C.O. A relationship between them was against the rules—could ruin her career. Hadn't she told him as much when they arrived here? After she discovered who he was.

He had kept away from her after that meeting, requesting an assignment as far from the capital as possible. It had been Julie, herself, who had sought *him* out. She had pursued him. Her cheeks flamed as she remembered the night of the carnival. She had initiated that encounter, too.

Except for their very first meeting, when he failed to identify himself as military personnel, he had always behaved honorably. Was he being honorable now?

What if he thought he needed to protect her by making sure no taint of scandal touched her? Was he trying to create as much distance between them as possible so that no one would ever guess the truth? Was he stepping aside for her career? Yes, that sounded like the Matt she knew.

And yet, knowing all he did about his reputation and how he was perceived by the senior command, he had come to her to request a promotion. No, she corrected herself, that wasn't quite right. Matt hadn't actually asked to be made head of the unit. He had merely offered to step in, an act that would be expected from the most senior officer in any unit that had lost its leader.

Had she been so disturbed by his cold demeanor that she had attributed motives to him that weren't there? Was her father right? Had she become so used to expecting the worst of people that she had allowed it to define all her relationships?

Oh, the things she had said to him. The accusations. She really *was* stupid. But not for believing in Matt. She was stupid for *not* believing in him.

She had to see him. She had to make things right between them no matter what. Even if it meant resigning her command.

Was she serious?

And then a glow of certainty engulfed her and she knew beyond all doubt where she belonged. It wasn't in an institution, no matter how much she loved it. The military couldn't keep her warm at night. It couldn't share her hopes and dreams. It couldn't let her be the person she longed to be. Only Matt could do that.

All thought of sleep forgotten, Julie hurried to her office. She had to talk to Matt. She'd call the barracks to have Corporal Marshall send him to her office.

As she reached for the phone, she saw her Browning lying on her desk. The telephone receiver remained in its cradle and she picked up the gun, her hand melding comfortably to the familiar form. She stared at it in disbelief. She had thought to never see it again. Did this mean...?

"Madame Major!" Suzanne rushed into the office, her speed so out of control she almost crashed into one of the red velvet chairs. "Have you heard?" she asked, gasping for breath. "They have caught the man who shot Captain Wilkes. And do you know who it is?"

Julie gave Suzanne an indulgent look. The girl was clearly bursting with the news. Julie's own heart had started beating a quick tattoo in her chest. The reappearance of her gun, a nine-millimeter, at the same time as they had caught Wilkes's attacker had to mean...oh, no, not her own gun!

"Well!" Suzanne interrupted her thoughts. "Shall I tell you?"

"Please."

"Jimmy the cook! I told you he was a bad man. *Phew*. Goodbye to Jimmy!" Suzanne looked very pleased with herself.

"Jimmy?" Julie was stunned. But as she began to unravel the intricate threads—from the appearance of the *vèvès*, to her kidnapping and, finally, the attack on Wilkes—it made sense. "But how? Who?"

"Ah, I see you beat me here," Murray said to Suzanne, as he entered the room. Always the perfect soldier, he stood to attention and saluted Julie, waiting for her acknowledgement before coming closer.

Julie suppressed a smile. He, too, looked as if he would burst with the news.

"Suzanne tells me that it was Jimmy who shot Captain Wilkes. But I think there's more, isn't there?"

Murray looked deflated, and shot Suzanne a look of annoyance.

"Suzanne, please sit. You're making me nervous with all your hopping about. You may sit, too, Master Sergeant." Julie signaled the small grouping of chairs she preferred for meetings.

"No, Madame Major. With your permission I will go tell the others about the capture of the bad man." Suzanne skipped from the room.

Comfortably settled, Julie turned to Murray. "Jimmy was behind the *vèvès* and my kidnapping, wasn't he?"

"Yes, ma'am."

"Okay, I know who. Now, can you tell me how?

How was he discovered and captured?" She paused, suddenly panicked. "I assume he's been taken into custody."

"Oh, yes, ma'am. We have him locked up."

"Good," she said, relieved. "Go on."

Even before Murray began, she knew who had been responsible for uncovering the identity of the Hougan and capturing Jimmy. Once again Matt had come to her rescue.

"It was Lieutenant Wolf," Murray said. "I guess he'd gotten some key information from a couple of the mambos—one here and one in Cap-Verte. He put it all together and then confronted Jimmy, on his own. I don't know why he didn't tell us when we were interro—ah, debriefing him last night. It meant Jimmy had the run of the compound pretty much the whole day. Thank God nothing else happened. He's a cocky fellow."

"Jimmy?"

"Lieutenant Wolf."

"Oh." She felt her heart soar. It was all she could do to remain seated and composed in front of Murray. Matt had captured the Hougan. She was safe.

"Only after he caught Jimmy did he bother explaining everything. The General was plenty pissed, let me tell you. Sorry, ma'am."

"That's all right, Master Sergeant. I've seen the General plenty pissed before. I've even been the cause of it, more times than I'd care to remember."

Murray smiled, visibly relaxing. "Yes, ma'am."

Julie wanted to hear more about Matt but recognized this as a good time to confront Murray about his mission for her father, and his allegiance to her.

"I would think that in all your years of service to my father you've seen him plenty pissed a time or two yourself."

Murray blanched; his mouth opened and closed several times. He seemed incapable of speech.

Julie couldn't hide her satisfaction at unsettling the usually unflappable soldier. "It's all right, Master Sergeant," she said kindly. "My father and I have discussed the situation. I understand you were only carrying out his orders. You may continue with his assignment to quell rumors and such, but from here on in, you are to report only to me. Is that clear?"

"Yes, ma'am."

"Good. Now, back to the other matter. I noticed my gun has been returned. Presumably Jimmy had it?"

"Yes. Lieutenant Wolf removed it from him when he was taken into custody."

"Is it...?" Julie really didn't want her suspicions confirmed, but she felt compelled to ask. "Is it the weapon that was used against Captain Wilkes?"

"I'm afraid so, ma'am."

"Shouldn't it be evidence, then?"

"It is. However, Jimmy has confessed to the attack on Captain Wilkes, and to your kidnapping. Therefore, the trial will be brief, little more than an allocution. Your gun won't be needed as evidence. Lieutenant Wolf insisted it be returned to you immediately."

Matt, again, looking out for her. He knew what the Browning meant to her and how its loss had devastated her.

Why would Jimmy confess? She was relieved, of course. If there wasn't a trial, she wouldn't have to testify about her abduction. The matter would be effectively closed as far as the military was concerned. Somehow, Julie knew, Matt was behind that piece of good news, too.

"I'd like to speak with Lieutenant Wolf." Julie rose, signaling the end of their interview. "Can you ask him to come to my office?"

"I'm afraid that's not possible, Major." Murray wouldn't meet her gaze. "He's left the compound, and the General has told me and the rest of his unit not to expect him back."

CHAPTER 12

Matt breathed in the damp, heady air as the jeep bounced along the dirt road away from Port-au-Paix and the military compound. The feeling of liberation was overwhelming.

In the back seat, James kept up a steady stream of youthful conversation, one arm wrapped affectionately around his tolerant pet.

Matt glanced at the woman beside him. She sat stiffly, her mouth sternly set, her gaze never wavering from the road ahead. Marie was the only one who seemed unhappy about their journey. Matt reached over to squeeze her hand reassuringly. She turned to face him and managed a wan smile.

He couldn't blame her for being anxious. He understood her concerns for both her son and herself. He had explained that with the Hougan in custody and his followers being rounded up, she had little to fear by returning home. He was certain Mama Sophie would welcome the return of her only grandson and his mother. But Matt would stick around just to be sure.

He smiled, recalling his conversation with the General. It had gone much better than he had anticipated. He had told him the whole story about Julie's kidnapping and rescue—leaving out the part about making love to his daughter, of course. The General had been angry and had lectured him on the chain of command, but agreed that the end result was probably better than would have been achieved otherwise. Nevertheless, both knew Matt's military career was over.

He thought it would be more difficult to walk away from the only home he'd had since his mother died—even before, if he was honest with himself.

The General accepted Matt's resignation with conditions. While the paperwork was making its way through the system, Matt would undertake a special assignment—one that would utilize his unique skills. With stability returning to Beljou, the aid agencies were clamoring to get back into the country to help its people rebuild their lives and livelihoods. Matt would serve as the military liaison between these groups until the troops completed their mission and returned to Fort Bragg. His new position would allow him to travel all over the island, helping to co-ordinate aid where it was needed most. But most importantly, Matt now reported directly to the General. Julie was no longer his C.O.

It hurt to think about Julie. Matt wasn't sure how he could make things right with her. She had been so angry and disillusioned with him. How could she think those things about him? He felt a charge of anger race through him, but it quickly turned to despair. He had to let her go. It would be so much easier for her, if she thought badly of him.

The jeep climbed the hill and the little community came into sight. He felt Marie stiffen beside him while James let loose a whoop of joy. While he may have enjoyed his time with the soldiers, he was happy to be going home.

A swarm of excited children raced to meet them as they entered the village. Their excitement grew when they saw James sitting like a king in the back of the jeep.

The women and a few men headed towards them, more cautious in their approach. It was almost curfew, so the arrival of a military jeep carrying local Beljouans was a cause of some concern. Mama

Sophie watched from her doorway.

Matt got out of the jeep and, carefully wading through the children, went to Marie and offered her his hand as she disembarked from the vehicle. Slipping her arm through his, he passed through the group of villagers and headed towards Mama Sophie. The enormous woman stepped aside, allowing the two to enter her home. James had already run off with his friends.

Matt allowed his eyes to adjust to the dimness. As his gaze took in the long table resting against the wall and the drawing of a mounted snake hunter above it, it surprised him that Mama Sophie's home was just as he remembered it. And why wouldn't it be? It had only been a week since his last visit—a week and a lifetime.

Mama Sophie descended into her favorite chair with a "harrumph" and motioned for Matt to do the same. Marie stood, eyes downcast, in the center of the room.

"Daughter, drinks, if you please." Mama Sophie finally broke the silence.

The woman jumped to obey.

"You, too," Mama Sophie said impatiently as Marie handed her and Matt their glasses of rum. She had only poured two.

Marie nodded, poured a glass for herself and sat down on a wooden chair close to Matt. She refused to look up.

"And so, Lieutenant Matthew Wolf, you are back. And I understand you were successful in your search for your Major?"

"Your sources are correct, Mama Sophie." Matt scanned the woman's face for some hint that she knew more than she was saying, but he could find none. She would make a worthy adversary in poker, Matt thought. "Do your sources also tell you that we've captured the person responsible for her kidnapping?"

Mama Sophie's eyes widened and Matt heard a sharp intake of breath. He smiled inwardly. This was news to her.

"I had not heard that," she said cautiously.

"Yes, I'm sorry to inform you that your husband will not be returning for quite some time."

"I see."

Was he imagining it or was he seeing relief in her eyes?

For the first time since their arrival, she looked directly at Marie. "And you, daughter? Are you and my grandson unharmed?"

"Yes, Mama," Marie's voice was a whisper.

"Good. When you disappeared at the same time as Lieutenant Wolf's Major, I feared the worst."

"No, Mama. James and I were safe with the soldiers. Lieutenant Wolf protected us."

"Well, Lieutenant Wolf," the woman turned back to Matt, "it seems I am in your debt. Daughter, more rum."

After refilling the two glasses, Marie escaped, ostensibly to see to her son. Matt didn't blame her. He was finding Mama Sophie's scrutiny unnerving.

"You have been on a great journey, Lieutenant."

"Yes, Mama, to Cap-Verte and back."

"That is not the journey I refer to."

"Oh?" Matt shifted uncomfortably in his seat.

The woman leaned towards him, bringing her eyes mere inches from his own. Matt willed himself to remain immobile. It seemed an eternity of seconds before she sat back. "Yes, a great journey—many years—and yet with the end so close you refuse to take the last steps to your final destination."

"Are you a fortuneteller now?" Matt asked, trying to break the tension he was feeling. "Shouldn't you be reading tea leaves or my palm, at least?"

Mama Sophie snorted scornfully. "Tricks! What I

need, I can find in your face, Lieutenant Matthew Wolf. It is the eyes that tell the story."

"No offense, but I don't need my future told to me. I know what it is."

She sighed heavily. "And still you run away from what you have always sought."

"I am not running!" He leapt to his feet. "I've resigned my commission. I've found the type of work I really want to do, and I can do that without the authoritarian bureaucracy of the military, that's all."

Mama Sophie's face remained impassive as she watched him pace around the room. It drove him nuts.

"It's better this way," Matt continued. "She's a far better officer than I am. It's what she wants to be. It means everything to her. I can only hold her back." He didn't know why he was telling Mama Sophie this. He didn't owe her an explanation.

"A job is not a home," Mama Sophie's deep voice cut into his rationalizing. "You have spent your whole life looking for where you belong. You have found it with your Major. Why now, at the end of your journey, do you shy away from its completion?"

"You're not listening. I can only hurt her career."

"You are the one who is not listening, Lieutenant Matthew Wolf. If you will not listen to me, then listen to what your heart is telling you. Have you not already done all you can to help your Major's career? Have you not already set in motion the events that can bring you together? You fail to see what all around is telling you. She is the home you seek. You must go home."

Home? Yes, thoughts of Julie brought with them a sense of peacefulness, a sense of belonging he'd never known before and had thought never to have.

While we might explore on our own, we prefer the company of others.

Could Mama Sophie be right? Was there a way

for them to be together? Had he already set in motion the events that could make it so?

Beljou was a minor operation involving a relatively few number of troops and, although Julie was well known, thanks to her famous family, it was unlikely many in the military would even know about her kidnapping. The Hougan's confession meant there wouldn't be a lengthy trial. The events of the past week would quickly fade from the memories of those few who were aware of them. And now that he'd resigned, Julie was no longer his C.O. The largest obstacle to their being together had been removed.

Blonde-hair, blue-eyes is not for you, Boyo. His mother's words no longer had the power to deter him. She was wrong. Blonde hair, blue eyes was *definitely* for him.

"Ah, yes, Lieutenant Matthew Wolf, you are at the end of your journey. You are home, at last."

"Not quite, Mama Sophie. I still have to convince the lady."

****

Julie stared out of her office window, oblivious to anything other than her own wretchedness.

She had sent word to her father that she couldn't join him for breakfast. He was concerned but for once didn't push. She snapped at Suzanne when the young woman tried to press some food on her. She'd have to apologize to her later.

What was happening to her?

The only peace she found since hearing that Matt had left was the few hours of sleep she had managed. She'd been certain, when she had crawled into bed, that her misery would keep her awake. But her body required sleep and so, remarkably, her mind gave in to the physical demand and allowed her to briefly forget.

It had been a deep, dreamless sleep designed to

heal her body. When she awoke she felt physically renewed. Her spirit was another matter, however. The awareness of Matt's absence immediately invaded her senses, causing her stomach to lurch and the band around her heart to tighten painfully. It was an emotional pain so deep she wasn't sure she could rise from her bed. She did manage to get up, somehow, to shower and make her way to her office.

The day was bleak. Rain pounded steadily on the windows, reminding Julie that yesterday's sunshine was only a brief reprieve. Beljou's rainy season was well and truly underway. The gloominess only added to her mood.

He's gone and he won't be back, Murray had said.

Matt left before she had a chance to talk with him. A few hours ago she'd been so optimistic they could work things out, believing that she had misjudged him. Apparently, Matt didn't want to work things out with her. How could he have just left her without saying anything?

Wait a minute! Soldiers can't just leave. If he was planning on going anywhere he had to go through her, his commanding officer. Unless...?

Unless he went to a higher authority. Anger bubbled inside of her, displacing the hurt.

"Damn him to hell!" Julie slammed her fist down on the desk and reached for the phone.

"I hope you don't mean me?" a voice said from the doorway.

Her head shot up at the sound of the familiar, slightly mocking tone. Inside her, a battle raged—relief fighting with despair, hurt fighting with anger.

Matt stepped into the room. He was dressed in formal military regalia, his maroon beret twisting in his hands. His eyes bore into her as if he couldn't get enough of her. Julie squirmed under the scrutiny. And then he gave her his slow, sexy smile and her heart stopped.

Finally, he tore his gaze away and turned to close the door. The few seconds allowed Julie to gather her wits. She inhaled deeply.

You're his C.O., Jules. You're the one in charge here.

"Did you forget something?" The tremor in her voice belied her attempt to sound sarcastic.

"Excuse me?"

"I thought you'd left. I was told you weren't expected to return to your unit."

"Ah, that."

"Yes, *that*! I think you owe me an explanation. How is it that you can leave your post without my permission? Don't answer that. I know. The General has taken it upon himself to remove you. Does he think me incapable of carrying out my duties?"

Julie rose from her desk and began pacing. She didn't know which she found more upsetting—Matt's presence here or the fear that her father had interfered.

Matt regarded her silently while she waged her internal war. Finally, she decided to deal with Matt. He was here and now. She'd confront her father later.

"Well, Lieutenant? Explain yourself."

"Julie." He took a step forward, but her look of reproach stopped him from moving any closer. He paused, seeming to reconsider his approach, and then stood to attention. "Yes, I went to the General and asked to be discharged. I knew he was angry with me, and I knew he didn't trust me. So I told him it could be either honorable or dishonorable—his choice—but I wanted out."

"Why?"

"We both know I'm not really suited for this type of work. It was fine before. I didn't really fit in anywhere and this was what I knew. I could make myself fit in. It's been getting harder, though. The rules, the regulations... I know they're needed. I just seem to be having more trouble with them... now." Matt spoke softly, his gaze never leaving Julie's face. "Yesterday was the final straw. Your reaction to my offer to lead the unit finally convinced me that I've been deluding myself. If you, the person who knows me better than anyone else in this world, don't see a place for me in the military, how can I stay?"

"You went to my father instead of me about this." It was an accusation.

"Yes. You were so angry. How could you think I would use you like that? After everything..." Matt's voice caught and he shook his head slowly.

His whole body seemed to sag and she could tell he was hurting. As angry as she was, she couldn't bear to see him in pain. "I'm sorry," she whispered. "I... I'm so sorry."

She didn't realize she was moving towards Matt until she found herself standing in front of him. Mere inches away from the sharp angle of his cheekbones, her fingers itched to trace their smooth line down his cheeks to his strong jaw. She breathed in his scent—she loved the smell of him—and a shiver escaped her. Even now, hurt and betrayed, she wanted him as she had never wanted anything before. Heat coursed from her belly, sending a fire of anticipation between her legs. She could see her own passion echoed in his eyes.

Let it go! her body screamed, desperate to feel his arms around her, his lips and tongue on her burning flesh.

She couldn't. There was still too much between them—too much left unresolved. Julie dropped her gaze and stepped away.

"After all the terrible things I accused you of, you still went and found the Hougan. You got my gun back. You fixed it so there wouldn't be a trial. Why?"

"All I've ever wanted is for you to be happy—to

pursue your dreams. If there's no trial, all this—your abduction, my disreputable conduct, all of it—will be quickly forgotten."

"But how did you get Jimmy to confess? It's surely in his best interest to have a trial. I mean, as Hougan he was looking for followers—for power. What better way than to take on America? Why would he give up the chance to be a martyr?"

Matt shrugged. "Persuasion. It's what I do. And I'm very good at it."

"Modest, too." She couldn't help herself, but softened the rebuke with a smile.

He chuckled, and her heart flipped at the sound. She cursed her traitorous body for making it so difficult to maintain her distance from him.

"Getting back to the General," she said quickly, trying to divert herself from running into his arms. She knew he cared for her—that was obvious from his actions. Everything he did seemed to be aimed at helping her career. Was that all it was? Was she a fool to think he might want more? *Don't go there, Jules.* "I'm assuming that since you're still in uniform he refused your offer to accept a dishonorable discharge. Did you employ your powers of persuasion on him, too?"

Matt had visibly relaxed. His beret was no longer in danger of being turned into a pretzel, and his eyes were full of humor. *He's enjoying this,* Julie realized with annoyance.

"I'm not sure that even my considerable powers of persuasion are much use against a man like the General. No, after a few choice words—which I won't repeat, but you can use your imagination—his reply was that a dishonorable discharge would undo all the work I'd done to save your reputation."

Julie stiffened. Save her reputation, indeed.

Before she could respond, Matt continued. "He also said," he paused dramatically, "that he refused to have any daughter of his married to a man with a dishonorable record."

It took a few minutes for the words to sink in. "You told him we were getting married?"

"I didn't have to. He's a smart man. He figured it out pretty quickly on his own." Matt paused, and then continued softly. "You know, it's funny. I'm pretty good at what I do, and a lot of that is because I can hide my thoughts and feelings from others. But in the past twenty-four hours, two people—your father and Mama Sophie—have both been able to see what I wanted, *what I needed*, better than I could." He reached out his hand to brush Julie's stray bang from her face.

"We can't get married!" Julie cried turning away. What was he thinking? Her heart was beating wildly and her head was telling her to slow down. This was happening too quickly.

"Why not?"

"Well, let's see. Maybe because I'm your C.O.?"

"But you're not."

Julie whirled around at his words. Damn him! He was calmly regarding her like a patient parent with a willful child. Well she wasn't a child. She was an adult. She was a major in the U.S. Army—responsible for over one hundred soldiers.

"What do you mean, I'm not your C.O.? My father may have agreed to an honorable discharge, but it doesn't happen that quickly. It could take weeks for the paperwork, and until then your ass is mine, Lieutenant."

Matt's eyes widened at the vehemence in her voice. "Actually, no," he said slowly, eyes dancing with mirth. "While I will gladly give you any part of my anatomy that you wish, my ass, figuratively speaking, is your father's."

As Julie opened her mouth to protest, he held up a hand to silence her.

"Your father has given me a special assignment. And until my discharge comes through, I'm to report directly to him."

"A special assignment?"

"Yes. I've been made special liaison between the military, the Beljouan government and the incoming aid agencies. It will allow me to really help the people here and ensure they get the kind of support they need to rebuild their lives."

Of course. It was the perfect assignment for him.

"Look, Julie, your career is important to you. Well, you're important to me. If I'm not in the military, we don't have an issue. We can be together."

He stepped closer and raised a hand to cup her face. His thumb slowly stroked her cheek. At his touch she felt the air rush from her lungs, and she struggled to breath.

"But, your career," she gasped.

"I'll just have to make *you* my career, won't I?"

"Don't be flip. This is important."

"I know. I can continue to do what I'm doing, just not with the military. Besides, the General has even hinted that I may be able to continue as a liaison once I become a civilian."

"My father again!" It always came back to him. *Why can't he just stay out of it?*

"The other advantage of leaving the military," Matt said quickly, "is that *he* won't be my C.O., either."

"He'll still be mine," Julie replied bitterly.

"You've got to let it go, Julie. No matter what you do, he'll always be your father. Allow him that."

"I know." She blinked frantically, trying to hide the tears welling in her eyes. It didn't work. Matt gently brushed away a runaway droplet. "I just want to be recognized for myself."

"And you think you're not?" There was genuine

surprise in his voice. "I've served with a lot of units and I can tell you, soldiers don't respect their C.O.s based on who their fathers are. The boys here respect *you,* and that is respect that you, and you alone, have earned."

She nodded, her mind and heart finally accepting what he was saying. Based on their conversation last night, she had to admit her father's behavior was less that of a meddlesome senior officer than of a concerned parent. He hadn't interfered with her career, but he was treading very close to doing so with her personal life. She'd take that up with him later. In the meantime, she turned her attention back to Matt who was gazing at her, adoration in his eyes.

"You've spent more than half of your life in the military," she said. "How can you just walk away from it?"

"Surprisingly, it's really not that difficult. All my life I've done whatever it took to fit in, even though I knew I never really did—until I met you. I don't know what spirits were at work that night I met you, but from the first moment I saw you I felt a peace I'd never known. I didn't want to let it go. Then, when I realized how my actions could hurt you, I tried to stay away. Even yesterday, I resigned my commission to stay away from you."

"But you came back," Julie's voice was barely a whisper.

Matt smiled ruefully. "My life was empty until I met you. Now that I know what it can be like, I can't go back. When I think about my future I know beyond a shadow of a doubt that it is with you—wherever you are, whatever you do. I've never felt like I belonged anywhere before. I love you, Julie. You are my home. Please don't send me away."

"I don't know," she moaned, finally allowing her fingers to stroke his handsome face. Could this really be happening? He said he loved her. He loved *her*, Julie Collins *the woman*, not Julie Collins the Major, not Julie Collins the daughter of the Army Chief of Staff. She had wanted this so badly—had even contemplated giving up her own career to make it happen—she could hardly believe the words she was hearing. "Oh, Matt, I love you too, but..."

"Shhh! No buts," he laid a finger across her lips to silence her protest. "Besides, I can be very persuasive," he said huskily, lowering his head and brushing his lips tentatively across her temple and down to her mouth.

Slowly, he caressed Julie's lips with his own. It wasn't enough. She grabbed his head, her fingers weaving through his longer-than-regulation silky black hair, and pressed him firmly against her. She opened her mouth, accepting his tongue, stroking it with her own. Her hips ground hard against him and she could feel his arousal pushing back.

"Convinced yet?" he asked, raising his head.

"Not quite," she said, smiling mischievously.

Matt laughed and bent to begin an exploration of the contours of her neck.

Eyes glazed with passion, Julie saw her door open and Suzanne bound into the office.

"Oh, *mondu!* Excuse me!" the startled girl exclaimed before turning, red-faced, to race from the room, slamming the door behind her.

Matt and Julie exchanged startled looks before bursting into laughter.

"Well, I guess that settles it," she said. "It'll be all over the compound before you even leave this office!"

"Are you okay with that?"

Julie gazed into his eyes. "Yes." And to her surprise, she realized she really was.

"In that case," Matt said, lowering his head to claim Julie's lips once more, "I think we should give Suzanne time to make sure *everyone* in the compound knows."

"Uhmm," she murmured savoring the taste of him. "There's just one thing."

"Oh?"

"I'll be expecting a proper proposal before you leave this office."

"Is that an order, Major?"

****

The sun had risen high in the sky. It was going to be another beautiful October day in Beljou. After suffering through the rainy season and the searing heat of summer, the troops of Company A were leaving the island just as it was entering its most temperate period. Within a few weeks, its beaches would be crowded with tourists escaping the harsh North American winter. Most would be completely unaware of their military's role in keeping the country safe.

Julie sighed, imagining herself relaxing on one of those beaches, as she looked down the lines of men standing at attention beside the Hercules aircraft. She had delivered her final address to the company and there had been a formal handoff to the new commander and troops. The only thing left was the ceremonial inspection before departure.

She remembered her review of the troops just before they had left for Beljou. There would be no surprises today. She knew all of the soldiers here, and spoke a word or two to each of them.

She paused in front of the four recons. They were easy to identify in their maroon-colored paratrooper berets. She had a soft spot for them and smiled warmly at Lieutenant Brownwell, Corporal Marshall and the two men who had been brought in to replace Wilkes and Matt.

Wilkes had made a full recovery from his attack, and she had just learned he would be waiting for them when they landed at Pope Air Force Base. The men cheered when she gave them the news.

Inspection completed, she watched the troops board the plane before climbing in herself. The pilot slid the hatch door in place and lowered the long metal security handle.

Julie slid into her seat beside the handsome man in civilian clothes who was her husband.

"I appreciate the lift, ma'am," he said, a twinkle in his eye.

"Think nothing of it, *Mister* Wolf," she replied. "After all your assistance these last few months, I think the least the military can do is get you home—even though using military planes to transport civilian personnel is strictly against regs."

"I hope it won't be a stain on your record," he said in mock horror.

"Considering all the regulations that I've broken on this mission, this one won't even make a mark."

She laid her head on Matt's shoulder. It had been a strange mission, indeed. Although she'd been somewhat worried about the reaction of the soldiers to her relationship with Matt, all of them—including her father—seemed to accept it as a matter of course.

It had taken almost two months for Matt's discharge to work its way through the system. As soon as it did, Mama Sophie had married them in a traditional Beljouan wedding ceremony. They had chosen the chapel on the palace grounds so that as many of the soldiers could attend as possible. Suzanne had served as her maid of honor and Lieutenant Brownwell had been Matt's best man.

Julie's father had already flown back to Washington by this time, but she was sure he'd received full coverage of the event from Murray. Despite his promise, Julie suspected the wiry soldier still provided reports to the General from time to time.

"Your parents will be meeting us when we land," Matt said.

"Really?" Her head jerked up in surprise. Of course, a lot of the General's information could be coming from Matt, she reasoned. He still reported to him—although now as a civilian contractor.

"Yes. He's also arranged for your brothers to be available for the wedding."

"What wedding?" Julie had to yell as the engines roared to life. Maybe she had heard him wrong.

"Our wedding," Matt said, the humor in his dark eyes thwarting his attempt to appear serious.

"But we're already married!" Julie was indignant.

Matt couldn't hold back his laugher at her outraged expression. "Yes, we most certainly are," he said when he caught his breath. "However, the Army Chief of Staff doesn't think a Beljouan ceremony conducted by the local mambo is good enough for *his* daughter. He wants a proper wedding—a full military, *and family*, affair."

"For someone who's promised to stay out of my career, he seems to have a lot to say about my personal life," Julie huffed. Surprisingly, though, it didn't bother her. "All right, then," she acquiesced. "But it better be fast. I don't want to wait any longer than necessary to reap the benefits of being Mrs. Major Julie Wolf."

"Trust me," Matt said meaningfully, his eyes smoldering. "There will be no waiting."

He lowered his head and pressed his lips softly to hers. The impact was electric and she wrapped her arms around his neck, delighting in the sensation.

A roar of "hurray" erupted from the cabin behind as the great Hercules lifted off the runway.

Wheels up. They were going home.

About the author...

Reading romance has been a big part of my life. Now that I spend much of my day writing business documents, I savor the opportunity to allow my creative muse to run free by writing them. I rarely go anywhere without a book; it makes unexpected delays more enjoyable. I am thrilled to think that one of my books may make someone else's day that much more pleasant.

I live in Ottawa, Canada, with my wonderful husband, two fabulous children, and a Siberian Husky who wishes it was winter all year long.

Visit Brenda at http://www.brendagayle.com

Printed in the United States
143973LV00004B/17/P

9 781601 544018